Chapter One

The conductor came along the 696 trolley bus, his ticket rack in his hand.

'Fares, please. Any more fares?'

A woman asked for a tuppenny to Bexleyheath, the conductor punched her a ticket, and moved on to a scruffy boy who was staring out of the window as if he was counting the bricks in the wall of the Woolwich Arsenal.

'Oi! Sonny. You deaf? I said, "Fares, please".'

Jack Bell didn't blink. 'So?'

'So, where you going?'

'Middle Gate. Told you, on top.'

'You done what?'

'Upstairs. Asked you for a penny half.'

'Did you now? So what are you doing down here if you paid me for a penny half upstairs?'

'Too smoky.' Jack coughed, to show how smoky it had been. 'It's the pipes, not the fags ...' He cleared his throat, noisily.

'Watch out! No spitting. That's a five pound fine.'

A man across the aisle laughed at the conductor. 'If you can't get a penny you won't get five pound off him, mate.'

Jack turned to the man and tapped the side of his nose – *mind your own business!*

'Where's your ticket, then?' the conductor insisted.

'Ain't got one. You never give me one.'

'I what?'

'You never give me one.'

'I never give you one?'

'You put me money in your pocket, instead of in your bag.'

'I put your money in my pocket?'

'Who's deaf now?' Jack asked – just as the trolley slowed for a bus stop, and the conductor had to hurry to the platform at the rear to see passengers on and off – plus Jack, who slid round behind him and jumped onto the pavement.

'Don't you ever get on my trolley again!' The conductor shook his fist.

'Not likely. Not with an old crook like you on board!' And Jack took off towards the Arsenal munitions factory's Middle Gate. He was a stop short of where he had to go, but it was worth the extra run to save the penny fare his mother had given him. He'd got the conductor thinking Middle Gate, so jumping off sooner had tricked him nicely – just the sort of stunt he was good at pulling.

Inside the Arsenal, Jack's mother was half of a team of two, filling shell cases with Amatol explosive, Doris Bell tipping it in and Ivy Filer screwing the fuse.

'Nine hours of it – don't it make your arms ache?' Doris moaned.

'An' don't your hands stink of gunpowder? I'm scared to light the kitchen stove in case I go up the chimney.'

'Ha!' Doris laughed. 'Like a rocket. You could be our secret weapon.'

The two women lived in the same terraced house in Depot Street, near the Woolwich power station, a lump of coal's throw from the River Thames. Jack was twelve, his father a soldier whom Doris had never seen again after his regiment had left the barracks up the hill. She and Jack were on the ground floor, sharing an outside privy with Ivy and her daughter Shirley.

Shirley had been on that same trolley-bus with Jack, but he'd taken no notice of her. No one ever did. She was twelve, too, pale and thin, and hardly ever spoke – too 'drippy' to bother with. But today they had to meet their mothers to go to Powell's Bargain Clothing Store for pyjamas and a nightie.

For the big evacuation.

'He don't want to go,' Doris was telling Ivy as they washed their hands at the end of their shift. 'Says being evacuated means he won't be here to stick up for me if Hitler comes marching down the High Street.'

'I don't know what Shirley reckons.' Ivy was taking off her rubber-soled work shoes. 'She never says much about anything.' She turned and folded her arms at Doris, sure sign that she was about to say something frank. 'To be honest, Doris, I don't even know if I'll miss her.'

Doris let that go. 'It's all brewing up with ol' Hitler, that's for sure, the way our lot's getting the kids out of it. But a few bob to help pay for special bits and pieces wouldn't hurt. Pyjamas! Anyone'd think my Jack's going to fetch up with some lah-de-dah lord an' lady.'

'Huh! An' a nightie. What's wrong with a vest?'

Doris laughed. 'You ask your Wally, when he comes back from the army!'

Ivy shrieked. 'Be the least of his worries!'

Coming out of the filling shed, the two women joined the queue filing out through the Middle Gates, and started looking around in the crowd for Shirley and Jack.

It was August, and still bright; and despite the air raid shelters dug into some back gardens, south London seemed peaceful. Most people were more scared by the price of food than by a war starting and German bombs dropping.

But war broke out soon enough when Jack caught sight of his mother. 'I ain't goin' away wi' no school!' he told her. 'So you needn't think I am.'

Tactfully, Ivy pulled Shirley's arm and walked her on ahead.

'You're doin' what you're told!' Doris pushed him along the pavement. 'I'm the one who says what's what!' And he was forced to go where she steered him.

'Still ain't goin'!'

'We'll see, won't we?'

Soon Fred Powell and his shop assistant were pulling out cheap nightwear, slippers, and plimsolls to show to the two women; Shirley standing in a corner sniffing, and Jack scowling at anyone who caught his eye – until his mother tried to hold up a pair of pyjamas for size, and he turned his back.

'Wastin' your time. I ain't goin'!' he said to the shelves.

'Ta, Mr Powell. I'll 'ave these.'

'That's a good bit of cotton you've got there,' Fred Powell told her.

'Yeah – an' a right little toe-rag to wear it …'

* * *

8

In a couple of years Jack would be leaving Union Street Elementary School. He would work in the dockyard or on the roads; there hadn't been any go at the scholarship for him. He was in Mrs Rosewarn's class of bigger boys and girls, which she kept in line with her voice and her cane. They called her 'Stroker' because of what she wrote in the school punishment book: 'two strokes', 'four strokes', or 'six strokes'. But when it was only a 'one-er' she wouldn't bother with the book, just take a swipe at the culprit. A lot of the time this would be Jack. He thought school rules were for everyone but him, and he had a cheeky mouth that he couldn't keep shut. But he rarely missed school. He made sure he went every day because of what they fed him. According to the public health clinic he was 'all skin and bone', which entitled him to a free school dinner, and he wouldn't get that if he spent the day riding the Woolwich Free Ferry or feeding hay to the horses at the coal jetty. Anyway, he could start doing all that when the school went away on the evacuation. It would be like the holidays, because a notice on the school gate said the school would be closed to children who weren't evacuated. And Jack had made up his mind that he wasn't going. He was absolutely dead sure about that. He was a Woolwich boy, a Londoner, not some country kid who couldn't count beyond the six udders on a cow. And he'd meant what he'd said about any Germans landing. If he didn't protect his mother from Hitler, who would?

They'd had a practice for their stupid evacuation, going from the school to Woolwich Arsenal station, with Mrs Rosewarn marching on ahead of her class like a general. And that had told Jack something useful. Instead of marching them down the middle of the road like real soldiers she kept them to the side, near the kerb and close to loads of shop doorways. And she wouldn't stop the whole school evacuation to go fishing Jack Bell out of Woolworths, would she? So, as they marched past the store, he'd slip inside, run through, and dodge out of the back entrance. He'd get lost for a couple of hours, then go back home. Sure, he'd get a good hiding off his mother, but that would be the end of it, not a lot worse than a few strokes – which would be like paying his rent to stay in Depot Street until Hitler got beaten.

Chapter Two

National Evacuation Day was going to be tomorrow, on Friday 1st September – the day Jack was going to thumb his nose at the Prime Minister, Union Street School, and his mother. He might not be all that bright at school lessons, but he felt cocky about one thing – he could always have his own way when he was dead set on having it. And on that Friday he was *not* going to be evacuated with the school.

He felt bad that morning as he watched his mother packing him up to go – him knowing it was all a waste of time. But he was only doing it for her, wasn't he? She'd got hold of a small suitcase from somewhere. It had a tin handle and rusty metal corners, and it smelt of old socks. She lined it with a Daily Mirror, and put in his new pyjamas and plimsolls, a pair of pants, a pair of socks, half a bar of soap, his toothbrush and tooth powder, a pink comb – *pink!* – his gas mask in its box, and some squares of cut-up old sheets for blowing his nose. She'd be pulling all this out again before bedtime but there wasn't anything he could do about that. He just didn't make too much of a fuss about having to wear his raincoat on a warm, dry, day. She pinned his label onto it, giving his name, address, and school for anyone who needed to know. But there was no destination. That was a secret.

She showed him a postcard before she tucked it into a split in the lining of the lid. It had her name and address on one side with a penny stamp stuck in the corner. The other side was blank.

'You send me this when you get there, with your address, and the name of the lady where you're staying.'

Jack played along. 'Ain't got a pencil.'

'No. Nor you haven't.' She went to the mantelpiece and took the wooden family pencil out of a mug. 'Don't drop it and break the lead all through. Pencils don't grow on trees.'

'What if I can't spell stuff?'

'Ask the lady. Never be frightened to ask. And if she's not nice to you, I'll be down there like one o'clock!'

And she would, too, Jack reckoned.

Lastly, she showed him his food for the journey. Wrapped in greaseproof paper were a couple of sandwiches, the jam showing through where she'd laid it on thicker for once. 'That should see you all right.'

Yes, thought Jack, for my tea back here!

And that was it. He was ready to go. His mother stood and looked at him with her head on one side, as if that gave her the sort of view of him that other people would have.

'You'll do.'

Was she going to cry? It would be a waste of tears if she did.

But she didn't. She gave him a hug, and a kiss on the top of his head. 'It won't be long, Jack. You'll be back home before you know it.'

Too right, Jack thought. And he did his best to keep a straight face.

'So we'll get round to the school, and keep ourselves tight, eh? No blubbing.'

He nodded, and grinned. 'Don't worry. Going away's not gonna be a bother to me.'

The war with Germany wasn't officially 'on' yet, but that Friday morning Mrs Rosewarn looked as if she had the organisation to beat the enemy on her own. Mr Rivers the headmaster might have been in charge, but it was Jack's teacher who made sure things happened. While the head watched from the top of the school steps she lined up the school class by class in the playground, the Infants first.

'We must march at the pace of the slowest,' she shouted. 'Then no one will be left behind.'

Jack cleared his throat. 'That won't be proper marching,' he told his friend Freddy. *But it would be just the ticket for getting away.* If he missed his chance to drop out of the line he could start pushing from the back, wait for a pile-up, and dodge off while it was being sorted out. Just the job.

'Attention!' Mrs Rosewarn called. 'Parents!' she shouted to the adults, 'you will not be allowed onto the railway platform, and the police inform me that the street outside the station will be very busy. So now is the time and place to say your goodbyes. On the first whistle please go forward to your offspring, and on the second, come away. And no sob stuff. We are all doing this for the safety of the nation's future.'

She blew her whistle once, a short commanding blast, and the adults – mothers, a few fathers, some grandparents and older brothers and sisters – went into the lines of children.

'Be good.'

'It won't be for long.'

'Keep your pecker up.'

'And stick together.'

Jack's mother came over to him, with that hard look on her face she always had when she was holding things back. But, tricky boy that he was, the last thing Jack could do was put on a sad goodbye. His kept his mind on where he'd go all day: along to Bostall Woods, or over the ferry to the Victoria Gardens.

She ruffled his short-back-and-sides fair hair. 'Cheerio, then, Jack. Be good for whatever lady has the rotten luck to get you.'

'Yeah, OK.'

'An' remember your p's an' q's. We might not be rich, but you wasn't brought up on a winkle barge.'

'Yeah.' Jack felt bad; but it was all for her, really, wasn't it? He was only staying behind so that he could fight any German soldiers who came parachuting down on Union Street.

He could hear Shirley snivelling behind him, and Ivy from upstairs telling her to be a brave little soldier. Huh! Some soldier she'd be! She'd start crying as soon as the guard waved his flag.

Mrs Rosewarn's whistle blew again. 'Parents, back!' she shouted.

Obediently, the adults separated themselves from their children. And suddenly Jack realised that his plan might not work quite the way he'd hoped. Differently from on the practice day, Mrs Rosewarn didn't march at the front. She sent Mr Rivers to lead the procession while she sorted out the rest. She came down the lines of waiting children and did spot-checks on some of their labels. She tutted at a few spellings, and wrote 'bed-wetter' on one girl's label. Jack looked along the line of his own class. Those country people were going to get some weird kids in their houses. There was Alfie Birch with purple patches of scabies treatment all over his head; and stuck-up Wendy Smith who wouldn't hold hands with anyone, not even in Dancing; and Eric Platt, who had grimy bits between his fingers like most people get between their toes. Still, they probably weren't all perfect down the country, either.

Mrs Rosewarn got the rest moving-off in their turn, out through the school gate, up Depot Street – where Jack's and Shirley's mothers shouted goodbye – and along Powis Street towards Woolwich Arsenal station. Every step of the way Jack's eyes were all over for his chance to nip out of the line when they got to Woolworths – or this shop, no, this one, no, this – until, blow it! Who was this walking alongside the school party, clearing the way for the children? Only a policeman! He was right beside him, cutting off any chance of diving into a shop doorway.

'Left, right, left right, get in step, lads,' the bobby told Jack and his partner Freddy – and there he stayed, past Cuffs and Garretts and Woolworths and Sidney Ross Toys, and past every other shop where Jack could have dodged, all the way to the station entrance. He hemmed Jack in as if he knew which boy out of all of Union Street School was going to run off. And he didn't move away until Jack was inside the station, and down the steps onto the platform, standing waiting with the rest for the special evacuation train.

''Aven't been on a train before,' Freddy said. 'Gonna be good, ain't it?'

'Yeah.' But Jack didn't mean it. He wasn't beaten, not yet. Every black hole had a little chink of light. And Jack was someone who could slip a cucumber up his sleeve while the greengrocer blew her nose: a lot of people close their eyes, doing that. He could ask a baker for a loaf off the top shelf and slip a couple of cakes in his pocket while the man was turning and reaching. So there had to be some stunt he could still pull. He looked left, he looked right, he looked up and down. And suddenly there, sure enough, on the 'up' platform where he was standing, Woolwich Arsenal Station gave Jack Bell the gift of a little chink of light.

Stay on your toes, Jack, and stuff works itself out – it always does.

Chapter Three

They had all been told to use the lavatories at school before they lined up, but as soon as they were on the station platform and they saw the Gents' and the Ladies' lavatories a lot of them wanted to go again.

'I'm dying, Miss – it's urgent!'

'There's not time.'

'I'm nearly doing it already …'

'We've only just left the school.'

Mr Rivers quickly placed himself in the doorway of the Gents', and Miss Blake hurried into the Ladies', where she paid the first penny for the use of each cubicle.

'Don't let the door shut!'

'Get in, quick!'

'Don't be silly, Cynthia. We've all seen a pair of drawers before!'

Jack too his time. Even when the rush was over, he stayed where he was on the platform, looking up at the pigeons on the roof as if he was a fancier – right until the train came in.

Everyone cheered.

'This is a Special,' the platform announcer said. 'This is a National Evacuation Special for Union Street Elementary School.'

They cheered again. Some looked at one another with brave eyes; others cried. Rag dolls and small teddies were being squeezed and twisted in their hands. But Jack stood still. He waited until the last boy came out of the Gents' and Mr Rivers went to have a word with the station master. He took a quick double-check on Mrs Rosewarn who was already shouting, 'Entrainment – begin!' He watched as she held open a carriage door for children to start getting in, the signal for the evacuees to board all along the train. For a few seconds her back was turned, and suddenly, like a sparrow diving for a crumb, Jack left the line and followed a man into the Gents' lavatory. He pushed his pen knife down into a money slot on a cubicle door and slid inside, letting it lock. Now no one could get the door open, unless he opened it himself. So he was safe. No one could get him out. The train would go in a few minutes – and then he could go out onto the platform and make a song and dance about the blooming school leaving him behind while he was doing his business. *Jack Bell getting taken out of London to go and hide in the country? Not likely!*

He sat on the lavatory seat and lifted his feet, in case anyone looked under the door. But who on earth was going to do that?

'Jack Bell!' *Mrs Rosewarn was right inside the Gents' lavatory – and with a man in there.* 'Where is he? Where's that boy?' There was a loud rapping on Jack's door. 'Jack Bell! Come out of there! You're holding up the whole of Southern Railways!'

Jack heard a penny being put in the money slot, and he realised, too late, that he hadn't double-locked himself in. She could open up from outside. Now what was he going to do? Climb over the top into the next cubicle? Take his trousers down and sit on the seat properly? But, no! He wasn't having that. Trousers up or down, old 'Stroker' would still drag him out and shove him onto that train.

He had lost this one.

The door opened, and there she was, eyes like red hot ammunition. 'Out!' She grabbed him by the neck, pulled him off the seat, and ran him out of the Gents'.

The station master was holding open a carriage door.

'In!' She kept her grip on him, and clawed a hand under his backside to throw him up and into the carriage.

'All aboard!' she called back to the station master. 'Wave your flag.'

Immediately, the train began to pull out of the station. But there wasn't a seat for both Jack and Mrs Rosewarn, so she sat on him – literally, on his lap – for half an hour all the way to London Bridge Station.

London Bridge Station was in chaos that Saturday morning. If Mrs Rosewarn hadn't had a grip on him all the time Jack could have tried all sorts of tricks to get away. The place was packed with school evacuees lining up to get onto all sorts of different trains, so Jack could have torn off his label and lost himself in the confusion. He could have walked from London Bridge back to Woolwich, down the Old Kent Road instead of down the road to Kent. But when they changed trains for the one going to the country, Mrs Rosewarn kept hold of him as tightly as any policeman with a prisoner, and she sat on him again, all the way to where they were going.

To a place called Mardenhurst, somewhere a million miles from dear old Woolwich.

The train pulled in at a station and everyone got off – but that didn't mean that they were there. Outside in the street there was a line of single-decker buses and coaches with 'Maidstone and District' painted on their sides. Mrs Rosewarn gave Jack over to Mr Rivers and started filling them up with children.

'Villages,' Mr Rivers explained to one of the helpers. 'We're to be divided between different village schools.'

By the end of fifteen minutes Jack was in the last coach, back with Mrs Rosewarn. To his disgust Shirley Filer was in it, too; but he didn't have to sit next to her because the teacher quickly wedged herself in next to him – up the front near the driver, and Jack suddenly felt a first little lift. It was a bit like being on an outing at the seaside for the day. All the buses in London had black steering wheels, but this coach had a white one. The seats smelt of leather. And the driver was wearing a long summer coat and a pair of sunglasses. Jack's mother had kidded him that evacuation would be like a little holiday – well, perhaps she was right. If they gave him a good place to stay he might just give it a few days before he ran off back to London.

He looked out through the front as the bus drove along twisting country lanes and under low trees. But he couldn't see anything to tell him where they were going. After ten or twelve turnings Jack had to lean over and ask the driver. ''Ow the heck do'you know where you're goin'?'

'Don't distract the man,' Mrs Rosewarn snapped. 'He just knows, the same way you know the streets of Woolwich.'

'There isn't any signs,' Jack persisted. He knew

from films that country crossroads all had pointy sign posts.

'And that's for a very good reason. If the enemy descends by parachute they won't know where they are. The sign posts have been purposely removed.'

In his head Jack saw a string of German soldiers coming down on parachutes, their legs dangling and their rifles pointing. He made a little noise in his throat that he wished he hadn't.

'Hitler's spies would have had to be in place for a good few months before they'd be able to direct their troops through these byways.'

Jack looked at Mrs Rosewarn. This was good stuff she was talking. 'You mean there's spies already here?'

'All over the country. Planted here years ago.' She made them sound like trees. 'See, children, they're getting the harvest in – ' back to being boring again. On the other side of a hedge a tractor was pulling a machine that was cutting the corn. But Jack stayed watching the road as the coach turned down another narrow lane. Could he have remembered all these twists and turns if he was an English spy in Germany?

Too soon for him the coach stopped at one end of a long village street. On the opposite side there was a church and a graveyard, and out through the front Jack could see a shop, and a pub, but they had pulled up outside a building with a sign that said 'Mardenhurst Village Hall 1910' – a dead give-away to spies – and in front of it a lot of people were standing waiting. Some of them clapped, some of them waved, some of them frowned; but mostly they were keeping their faces tight.

The driver got up to open the bus door.

'Remain seated!' Mrs Rosewarn ordered the children – and the driver sat back down. He went red, and got up again.

Jack stared out at these people. They were all different sorts. So who would he fancy living with, if he did give it a few days? That woman in the black hat? She'd got a kind face, even if it did look a bit soppy. Or that younger one with a pram? No – babies always cry a lot. What about that tall man and fat woman leaning over the fence? But they were staring harder into the bus than Jack was staring out, moving their heads about to get a good eyeful of all the children, so he kept his head down. They looked as if they were up to some sort of business …

The driver opened the coach door.

'Seat by seat, on my word, you will proceed into the village hall,' Mrs Rosewarn said, 'and you will sit cross-legged on the floor with your belongings in front of you.' She turned to Jack. 'And you will stay where you are until I say so.'

The Union Street children started getting off the bus, all very quiet – except Cissy Jackson calming down her crying brother. 'We'll be all right, Tom. We're gonna be … all right.'

It was mid afternoon and the sun was still bright, but the villagers were squinting at the children. As they came off the coach and walked into the village hall they all got the once-over – especially from a tall woman holding a leather folder, who nodded and smiled at everyone as they walked past. When Jack's turn came this woman introduced herself to Mrs Rosewarn.

'I'm Edith Lewis, your billeting officer. Librarian, really, but needs must ...'

'How do you do? Mrs Rosewarn, Union Street School, Woolwich.'

'I have here a list of volunteer foster parents, most of whom are present. And I have a small car for the outlying homesteads.'

'Very good.' Mrs Rosewarn looked about her. 'Is the teacher from the village school present?'

'Not yet. Miss Buckshoot is attending to other matters pro tem.'

Mrs Rosewarn's mouth made it very clear what she thought about that.

'We can settle the children into their billets over the weekend, and enrol them into the school on Monday morning ...'

Mrs Rosewarn breathed in through her nose, quite noisily.

'... And I rather hoped you might do me the honour of sharing my small cottage with me ...'

'As you wish. Very kind.'

Jack had a sudden horrible thought. What if he had to go and share it, too? Old Stroker hadn't let him out of her sight all day.

She took Jack into the hall, where most of the children were already sitting cross-legged on the floor. She let go of him and clapped her hands for silence. Moving fast, he got himself as far away from Shirley Filer as he could and slid along the floor; the last thing he wanted was to end up anywhere near that grizzler.

The villagers had all followed in after Jack. Now some of them started staring or pointing at different children, but most just stood looking, their arms folded, reminding Jack of his mother when she was making up her mind about something. But not the tall man and the fat woman who had stared-in through the bus windows. They pushed themselves through to the front and the man stuck his arm out straight and pointed at two big boys, Rodney Bennett and 'Bully' Betts.

'We'll take them.' The man had a deep voice, a bit foreign, like some of those Jack heard in Woolwich, come over the ferry from the docks.

'In good time,' Miss Lewis said, taking out a sheet of paper. She stood facing all the adults, her back to the children. 'You may remember from when I came to see you that I am the billeting officer sent from County Hall, and I have your names and your available beds listed in alphabetical order ...'

'A, B, C,' Jack said.

'Exactly.'

But, 'Sorry,' said the tall man. 'Farm business can't wait all the way down to the "H"s. I have to get back to a barn of livestock.' He pointed to a name on the woman's sheet. 'Hunden. Red House Farm. And we can give a home to those two boys there at the back.' He pointed again. 'Stand up, then, you two.'

Rodney and Bully stood up, and Jack crouched as low as he could. The man walked over to them and gave them a good looking-over. 'Yes. This one and this one,' he said.

'Bennett and Betts, stand to the side,' Mrs Rosewarn commanded. She nodded to Miss Lewis to carry on. But now the fat woman stepped forward.

'And that girl there,' she said, pointing at Shirley

Filer. 'We can give a good home to three.' She sounded more 'country' than her husband.

Jack flattened himself even closer to the floor.

'But you only volunteered for two.' Miss Lewis was looking at her sheet.

'Well, we can take three. Do our bit, best way we can.'

Some of the other villagers started muttering.

'Well, that's very good of you, Mrs Hunden.'

Jack stared at Shirley. Just for once she wasn't snivelling, but was getting to her feet looking as if she was having a weird dream.

'Then gather your belongings, you three, and give your labels to Miss Lewis,' Mrs Rosewarn ordered. 'The labels are numbered,' she told her, and I have the code. Just note the numbers next to the names of the hosts.'

'Yes, thank you.' Miss Lewis did as she was told. 'And you're each to take a tin of corned beef from that box by the door to give to your hosts,' she told them.

But Mr Hunden and his wife were already picking up their tins and walking quickly out of the village hall – followed by the first three Union Street children to be billeted.

And as Jack watched them go, after feeling a bit more chirpy on that coach, he found that he'd got a rather nasty taste in his mouth.

Chapter Four

At the end of an hour it was nearly all over. All through, Jack kept thinking he was going to be picked by one of these people – just for a day or so before he cleared off back to Woolwich. Anyway, he was going to want to get his head down somewhere tonight. So when he saw someone he half-liked the look of staring in his direction he sat up with his back straight and his eyes wide open, the perfect boy to pick. And when he saw someone he took against – like a whiskery woman with a drip on her nose, or an old girl in gumboots covered with country cack – he leant over as low as he could and traced the grain in the floorboards with his fingers. But, head up or head down, no one wanted him. He had opened his big mouth with that 'A, B, C', and nobody wanted a cheeky cockney around.

The little girls all went first, then the Beckett family were taken by a woman with a nice smile. Then one by one the others went, even Alfie Birch and Eric Platt, probably because one looked as if he wouldn't eat very much, and the other was big enough to pull a cart. In the end there wasn't a tin of corned beef left in the hall – but Jack was.

Miss Buckshoot, the teacher from the village school, had come by now, who stood talking to Mrs Rosewarn. Miss Lewis – the one with the leather folder – had taken some lucky people off in her car and come back a couple of times, looking at Jack as if she wished he'd vanished.

Jack was starting to feel like the enemy: a captured German spy; or a parachutist who'd landed in a cart of horse dung. But he didn't let it get to him. He didn't feel lonely – Jack had never felt lonely in his life – but he did feel left out, like when everyone's allowed to play and he isn't, especially when he was the only one left in the hall out of a whole coach-load of Union Street kids.

Well, Jack reckoned, if he could get out of this hall with his little case – he'd still got some food in that, in a packet he'd lifted off a seat at London Bridge – he could track his way back to the station and worm himself onto a train. He stared through the door out to the village street, and freedom. But for the life of him he couldn't come up with an excuse that would get him through it. He looked at the door at the back of the hall, which led out to the toilets. But Mrs Rosewarn was on top alert over Jack Bell and lavatories. *So how could he get out of this place?*

It had all gone very quiet. Those three women were just standing looking at him. Mrs Rosewarn was wearing her smell-under-the-nose face. The other teacher looked as if she wouldn't touch him with a bargepole. And the leather folder woman was getting out her hankie to dab at her eyes.

But a new sound from outside had the three of them swinging round towards the door. It was a car, and from its engine it was a big one. One door slammed, then another, and suddenly a man was standing in the doorway. He was about the age to be a soldier, but he was wearing a black suit with a collar and tie.

'Lady Ashwell,' he said in a put-on voice. He stood

to one side, making way for a woman in a long coat and a silk headscarf which was tied under her chin.

'Hello,' she said. 'Sylvia Ashwell.' She stuck out her hand, which had a glove on it. Mrs Rosewarn went up to her and shook it.

'Mrs Rosewarn.'

Miss Buckshoot, the other teacher, bowed and said, 'Ma'am,' and Miss Lewis curtsied.

'I'm sorry to be late,' Lady Ashwell said. 'Sir John's on a leave weekend, and we'd promised ourselves that if the balloon hadn't gone up by today, we'd sort out the pond.'

'You can't let a pond run riot,' Miss Buckshoot said. 'War or peace, water lilies know no boundaries.'

Jack had once seen a pond. It was in the Pleasance Gardens in Plumstead, with goldfish the size of sharks.

'We were up to our hindquarters in waders and lost all sense of time.'

Mrs Rosewarn closed her eyes.

'So, what have we got left?' The lady looked directly at Jack, smiling at him and making him feel awkward. 'We must all play our part.'

Well, what they'd got left was him, Jack thought. And thinking about the fix he was in, a day or so in this lady's house would do him all right. He stood up and came to attention, his arms and hands hard into his sides, the way he did for drill.

'This is Jack,' Mrs Rosewarn told Lady Ashwell. 'But – '

'"Jack".' Lady Ashwell said his name as if 'Jack' was someone in a film. 'I've got a brother Jack.' She walked past Mrs Rosewarn and came across the hall. 'And what's your surname, Jack?'

Jack didn't know what she meant. He was Jack Bell, that was all.

'Your second name. Jack Who?'

'Oh. Bell, Miss. Jack Bell.'

'Milady,' Miss Buckshoot stuck in.

'Oh, forget all that,' Lady Ashwell said sharply. 'He can't "milady" or "ma'am" me all over the place like a servant. He's a refugee from a danger zone.'

But blow all that – Jack couldn't believe his luck. He was going to be taken off by this posh lady, in a big car from the sound of it – bigger than any of the other Union Street kids had ridden in. Or, was he? Lady Ashwell was looking at the label pinned to his raincoat.

'Is there anything I should know?' she asked him in a voice meant just for him. 'Do you wet the bed, or walk in your sleep, or act cruelly to cats?'

Jack shook his head.

Miss Lewis must have guessed things were getting personal, because she came across and said, 'All our evacuees have gone to their new abodes in good spirits, Lady Ashwell, a credit to their London school and to their parents; as I'm sure this young man will be …'

Mrs Rosewarn coughed.

'Splendid,' Lady Ashwell said, 'then we shall take ourselves off to the Hall. Chin up!' She led the way out of the village hall as Jack picked up his case and followed.

And – t'riffic! What a car! Jack wanted to whistle, the way workmen did at girls. It was a four-door Austin Cambridge Ten, gleaming black with a high polish. On the right hand front wing was a shining metal rod, the sort that would have an officers' flag on it, although it was bare right now. If one of these was seen flapping in Woolwich, soldiers in the street had to stand to attention and salute.

'This is Mr Parker,' Lady Ashwell told him, waving a hand at the man who was with her. 'Our handyman and driver. Mr Parker, this is Jack Bell, who's coming to live with us.'

'Ma'am,' Mr Parker said in that put-on posh voice again. He opened a rear door of the car for Lady Ashwell, and jerked his head at Jack to send him round to the other side, which was a shame, because Jack wanted to sit up at the front.

The man leant in and took Jack's case off him to put in the boot. As he did so, he bent forward to say something in his ear. Jack cocked it, ready for a friendly word.

'Don't push your luck, son!' he said, suddenly sounding as if he could have lived in Depot Street. 'I've got your number.' With a finger and thumb he gave Jack's ear a hard flick, which hurt. But Jack said nothing.

Lady Ashwell tapped his knee. '"Aunt Sylvia",' she said.

'What?'

'My name. To you. "Aunt Sylvia".' Say it, and start getting used to it, because I'm not having you "Mi'lady-ing" me all over the place.'

OK, thought Jack, that's no problem. He'd call anybody anything if there was a slice of cake in it. And it looked as if he might be in for a good bit more than that, so long as he kept out of the way of this horrible man.

He gave her what she wanted. 'Wotcha, Aunt Sylvia,' he said, feeling awkward as he said it, but with the sort of smile he thought she'd like – but which only made his ear sting again.

The car pulled away slowly and headed along the village street. They passed the 'Oak Tree' pub and a grocer's shop called 'Clarks' Stores'.

'This is The Street,' Lady Ashwell told him.

Jack was more interested in the car, though. He'd never been in a car before, and the special smell of it made it seem as if he was sitting in a different world. Posh. Everything was so *smooth*, it was like being a king in a procession. And those shiny, round, black dials made his mouth go dry.

'What's it called?' Jack asked, to be polite to the lady. 'This street?'

'"The Street".'

She didn't understand. Jack knew it was the street. The same as that was the shop, that was the pub, and over there was the church – but they were all supposed to have names, weren't they?

'No, *What* Street?' he asked.

'It's just called "The Street".'

'Oh.' Well, that wasn't very clever, he thought. Woolwich had hundreds of streets, and they'd managed to think up names for every one of them. This place just had one, and they couldn't come up with what to call it. 'I get you,' he said. But he didn't.

'And there's the school.' She pointed out to the left. 'You'll be enrolled there on Monday morning.'

Jack looked at the school. Unlike Union Street,

31

which had three floors and was one of the highest buildings in Woolwich, this was just on the ground, with red tiles on the roof.

'St James's Church of England Elementary School.'

'I'm not all that t'riffic at lessons,' Jack said, as a matter of fact. Not that he'd be coming to the school much after Monday; he'd be back in Woolwich soon.

'And here's the War Memorial ...'

They had come to the end of The Street, where there three ways to go: down a lane on the left; down a lane on the right; or on past the War Memorial where there were two wooden gates with small arches. One gate was wide enough for the car, and the other one was for people.

Mr Parker took the car straight ahead, and stopped it in front of the gates. He got out and swung the big gate open, then drove the car through, stopped again, and turned round to Lady Ashwell.

'P'raps the boy could give a hand, Ma'am?'

'Hop out, Jack, and shut the gate,' Lady Ashwell told him. 'Mr Parker's got a bone in his leg.'

Jack didn't need telling twice. For the first time since Woolwich he could stop being a parcel. He got out of the car, gave the gate a good shove, and jumped on it. 'Wheee!' – riding it in a wide arc until it shut with a clatter. He'd hardly got back into the car before Parker started off along a straight roadway with huge trees on either side, until they came to the door of a big, square, house.

'Here we are, Jack. Ashwell Hall. My home, the colonel's home, and your home, for the duration.'

Jack frowned. What was a *duration*?

'For the duration of the war.'

Mr Parker opened her ladyship's door but he left Jack to open his own.

'Now let's go inside and show the colonel and the children what I've bagged.' Lady Ashwell walked briskly up the front steps to the door – as Mr Parker threw Jack's case at him, and muttered, 'Take it yourself.'

But, *children*? No one had said anything about any children. And that thought brought him down, him having to fit in with other kids, even for a day or so – because if he reckoned he was anything, Jack Bell was a boy who did stuff on his own.

Chapter Five

Forget the posh house, as he went into Ashwell Hall it was the blackout screens that took Jack's eye. Today was the first day blackout had to be used, and back in Woolwich his mother had been going on about it – the job of stopping any light from shining out and guiding German aeroplanes to London. Someone in the Arsenal had sold her a pair of heavy curtains, and Jack had found her a big piece of cardboard she could stick up at the kitchen window. Otherwise, she'd said, they just wouldn't switch on any lights. But here in this big house the blackout leaning against the walls was like things they made in Woodwork. They were proper jobs. All the frames were planed and cut to size – with mortise and tenon joints, not nails – and tacked to them was stretched black canvas. It looked as if it was right ready to go up before dark.

Suddenly, a man poked his head over one of the frames. He had a round, red face, a small moustache, and bright eyes. 'What ho!' he said. 'You got us a London nipper, eh?'

Jack wasn't very happy with that; he was quite a decent size for his age.

'This is Jack,' Lady Ashwell told the man. 'Jack Bell. Not John. We shall call him "Jack", and he's going to call me "Aunt Sylvia".'

'As you wish,' the man said – who Jack guessed was the woman's husband. 'Well, the war balloon's going up in a day or so. You probably won't see too much of me, Jack. But when you do you can call me "Colonel". That'll suit fine. But no darned saluting, because I have to jolly-well salute back every time.' He came out from behind the blackout frame. Jack had thought he'd been bending down to do something, but he wasn't – he was just on the short side. He was wearing a pair of old baggy trousers, with his shirt hanging out, and khaki braces that had slipped off his slopey shoulders.

Straight off, Jack liked him. He didn't seem like a colonel at all, definitely not the sort of officer who marched to the front of the queue in the Post Office, or paraded along Powis Street in leather gloves.

'Light! It's got to be our night-time enemy,' the colonel said, lifting up a blackout frame. 'I've told the others. Don't trust the blighter. While you're masking the opening of a door with the biggest tarpaulin on God's earth, a drop of devilish light can slip out through the hinge side like escaping water. A sliver could do it, a *sliver* – then we've got the village policeman a'knocking, and Colonel Sir John Ashwell up in front of the bench.'

'I doubt that Jack will be opening the front door too often at night, Johnnie,' Lady Ashwell told him.

'All the same – as head of the household I've done my duty. Instructions given. Now,' he wrenched a tobacco pouch from his back pocket, and to Jack's surprise didn't fill a pipe but started to roll a cigarette. 'Quarters. Where are you putting Jack?' he asked his wife. 'I'll take him up and settle him in.'

'I thought, the Orchard Room.'

'Good thinking.' Colonel Ashwell finished his tobacco rolling, laid the unlit cigarette along the top of a blackout frame, reached out to Jack in a quick grab and took his case from him and started heading for the stairs. 'Come on, race you. Last one up's a cissy.'

'Johnnie!'

Jack chased after him – he was good at cutting corners – but the colonel baulked him and wouldn't let him past. So the man cheated and he won – which Jack didn't mind at all. He was starting to think he might give these people more than a couple of days – if things kept on like this.

Jack's room was very small but out of the window he could see some trees with what looked like red apples hanging on them. He'd get out there tomorrow and scrump some. The window had a blackout curtain already hanging in place – there was no need for one of the frames from downstairs. It was heavy and really black, on a rail that went far enough on either side of the window to let in plenty of light when it was pulled wide open. The bed was narrow and quite high off the ground – unlike Jack's camp bed in his mother's room – and next to it there was a hard chair and a chest of drawers with a speckly mirror on top.

'Nell's old room,' the colonel said, as he put Jack's case on top of the chest of drawers. 'Nanny Nell. Went off her rocker, poor old girl.' He pointed to a clothes hanger on the back of the door. 'Coat and jacket. Rest in the furniture.' He gave the chest of drawers a hard smack as if it was a horse. He looked down at Jack's legs and his school shorts. 'And if you pass fourteen before we've done for Adolf Hitler, I'll kit you out with a pair of long'uns.'

The colonel pressed down on the bare mattress on the bed.

'Good and firm – best for growing boys.' He frowned, seeming to register that the bed wasn't ready. 'I'll get Florrie to make up your bunk.' He took a final look around the room, and casually, one-handed, picked up the pillow – and suddenly whacked it around Jack's head.

'Hah!' he said. 'Gotcha!' and he dived out of the door.

She'd been hiding when he'd got there, Jack thought. She'd been giving him a secret looking-over, to be one-up – it was the sort of thing Jack would do himself. A bell had rung and he'd come downstairs – and there was this girl, standing in the hall. She was a bit older than him, suntanned, and she had dark hair tied with a ribbon. She was wearing a short frock, white ankle socks, and soft pink shoes – and she was pretty. As he got to the bottom of the stairs she came across the hall and shook Jack's hand.

'Hello,' she said. 'I'm Wendy.'

Jack knew he'd gone red. 'Wotcha.'

'You're Jack, aren't you?'

''S'right.'

'Pleased to meet you.'

'Ta.'

There was a sudden loud whoop as a boy jumped out of a cupboard door that Jack hadn't noticed.

'And I'm Clive!'

The two Ashwell children laughed as if a boy coming out of a cupboard was the biggest joke in the world. Jack sized him up. He was about his own age, a bit taller, with long hair that flopped down over his eyes. He was standing in front of him with his hands on his hips and his head back, laughing, the way the comics drew people laughing at jokes. Well, one punch on that snitching nose would soon put a stop to that. But Jack just stared him in the eyes, not blinking.

'What's in there?' he asked, nodding at the cupboard the boy had come from.

'Oh, brooms, and such. Mops. Buckets.'

''Cos you've got a whopping big spider on top of your 'ead.'

'What?' Clive gave a scream and jumped about, hitting the top of his head with his hands. 'Have I got it?' he asked Wendy. 'Get it!'

She just stood there, her mouth twisted. 'Nothing there,' she told him, giving Jack a cool look.

''E's gone down your shirt.' Jack wasn't going to let up.

Clive yanked his shirt out of his trousers and tried to get it over his head. 'Help! Help me!'

'Wasn't 'alf big,' Jack went on. 'You could fry it for your tea.'

Wendy still didn't move. She kept her face straight, didn't laugh at her brother's capering, but her look at Jack told him it was only out of loyalty. 'There wasn't one,' she said, 'Jack made it up. You've been had.'

Clive calmed a bit, started tucking himself in again. 'It's not because it's a spider,' he said, 'I'm not scared of English spiders, but Da's been out to India and he came back with foreign things in his luggage.'

Jack still hadn't moved. He'd seen to these two, he thought. The girl knew he'd won, and this Clive knew it, too.

'Spiffo!' Clive said, coming over to shake Jack's hand. 'Good jape. You got me there. I take my hat off to you.'

Only now did Jack unclench his fists.

'Oh, splendid.' Lady Ashwell came into the hall from the corridor that led to the kitchen. 'You've met. Well, Florrie thinks it's high time for tea. Have you all washed your hands?'

Jack hadn't. He shook his head.

'Use the lobby lav,' Wendy told him. She opened another door in the panelling, on the other side of the front door. Jack went in, and down a couple of steps to where a lavatory bowl sat beside a small wash basin.

'Lavatory, Wen,' Lady Ashwell was murmuring. 'Avoid "lav" where possible.'

'Don't use Da's face flannel for anything,' Clive called in, before Jack could lock the door. 'Ha, ha.'

The lobby lavatory had a small window, with its own blackout screen ready to be lifted into place. He decided to pee, just because for the first time ever he could do it indoors. What his mum called luxury, this was. But he wasn't going to get too used to it, oh no, because he'd always got her to think of her, first – for when those Germans came parachuting down on Union Street.

They had their tea in the kitchen – at the biggest table Jack had ever seen. It was served by Florrie – who, if she was a maid, didn't look like one to him. He'd seen maids in films, and they all wore white pinnies and little hats. This one wore the same as a lot of women in Woolwich, a flowery overall tied-up at the back. And instead of a little hat, her hair was just cut short. If she hadn't been wearing the overall she could have been a man. She was funny, though. She had a deep voice, and when she put the beans on toast in front of each person she said something different.

'Dover sole and custard,' she said to said to Wendy. 'Pig's trotters and toenails,' to Clive. And, 'Jellied eels and ear'oles for the boy from London.'

'Ta.'

Jack was hungry. He looked for the tomato sauce to go with the beans on toast, but instead of a bottle of ketchup there was a little dish with brown sauce in it, and a tiddly little spoon. He grabbed his cutlery, but before he could get his first forkful into his mouth Lady Ashwell came into the kitchen.

'Er-hum. Grace.'

Wendy and Clive closed their eyes and put their hands together. Jack did the same, just like in Assembly.

'For what we are about to receive, may the Lord make us truly grateful.'

'Amen.'

'Dive in!' said Jack, picking up his fork again.

'Bon appétit,' Lady Ashwell corrected.

With his free hand Jack dribbled the sauce all over his beans.

Clive and Wendy took some themselves, but put theirs in one spot on the sides of their plates.

'Napkins, Florrie,' Lady Ashwell said. 'We forgot the kitchen napkins. Now – ' she went to a drawer and took out three squares of linen. She rolled them up and slid them into wooden rings, each decorated with different sorts of cuts.

'What's this for?' Jack asked – straight away wishing he hadn't, because he could have watched the others. They took their napkins from their rings and spread them over their laps. *Oh, serviettes!* Napkins were serviettes, they had these in Lyons' Cafés. It was the wooden rings that had thrown him.

'Now, a bit of business,' Lady Ashwell said, sitting at the table and watching them eat. 'You'll have one bath a week, on a Friday, and good washes every other day,' she told Jack. 'Your sheets will be changed fortnightly, and washing day is on Monday, so all dirty linen is to go in the basket on Friday nights.'

Jack eyed his next forkful while he waited to say 'OK'.

'And it's house slippers or plimsolls indoors, shoe cleaning overnight in the scullery.' Lady Ashwell pointed to the room that lay between the kitchen and the porch to the back door. 'Any questions?' She was looking directly at him.

'Any more beans?' he asked.

'"Please".'

'Please.'

'And, no. We all have to get used to less protein. But we do have mopping-up hunks for hungry boys, don't we, Florrie?'

'Yes'm.'

Florrie started sawed off a couple of hunks of bread, but Jack was the only hungry boy – so he ate Clive's as well, mopping up every last trace of baked bean.

'Breakfast will be in here.'

What? That sounded years away. It was only six

o'clock, and he never went to bed before his mum started getting ready to go up.

'Tomorrow, being Saturday, we'll picnic if it's nice, and show you some of the village on the way.'

Jack kept his face straight. He'd seen the village. The Street. What else was there to see?

'And then on Sunday we shall lunch in the dining room, before Da – the Colonel – goes back to the unit. After church,' Lady Ashwell added. 'You do attend church?' she asked Jack.

'Sundays, mostly,' Jack told her. Well, that's what she wanted him to say, wasn't it? And he wasn't bad at singing: he usually did all right at Christmas-carol time, round the streets. The Lord's Prayer wasn't a problem, either: forget that any time, and old 'Stroker' helped you to remember. 'What time's that?'

'We go to the eleven o'clock,' Wendy told him. 'And Sunday School at three.'

'Gawd!' said Jack.

'I beg your pardon!'

'Gawd be praised,' he said.

'Indeed,' said Lady Ashwell. 'Splendid.'

Chapter Six

Jack was good at playground games – it was his best thing at school. People wanted him in their team. He had an eagle eye and fast feet. He could hit a rounder and be back at base before the ball came down off the roof of the school. And on the street he could beat any copper over fifty yards. So after tea he enjoyed the game in the grounds behind Ashwell Hall. Here he could run in a straight line until he got a stitch and still not come to a wall or a fence. Wendy was fast, too; she beat him in the eighty yards, but he won the two-twenty. Clive did more jumping up and down than running, but he was a good climber of trees, and in the big oak he went ten branches higher than Jack.

'Only because I know my route,' he said. 'All the hand and foot holds. I'll teach you.'

'Don' bother. I'll find me own.' Jack was good up drainpipes when balls got stuck, and fast over walls; and getting away from anyone he could drop down from higher up than most boys.

Clive stayed up his tree while Jack and Wendy threw a tennis ball at one another. They kept it up for over a hundred, harder and harder at each other, their eyes bright and their hands stinging, until Jack finally dropped it at a hundred-and-eight.

'Balls!' he said.

'I don't think we're allowed to say that, are we, Wen?' Clive called down.

'I don't think so,' Wendy said, 'but we shan't ask.

Best to avoid.' She came over to Jack and put her hands on his shoulders. 'I'm very glad that out of all the village you chose Ma.'

'Yeah,' Jack said, gruffly.

A small bell tinkled from the kitchen porch. 'Supper and bed-socks,' Florrie called. 'Wash your paws.'

Supper! No one had said anything about supper. So, what would it be, down here in the country? Scrambled eggs? Tomatoes on toast? He ran to the back door, threw his hands under a tap in the scullery sink, and headed into the kitchen.

Florrie was pouring hot milky stuff into three mugs, and in the middle of the table was a plate with biscuits on it. Three biscuits. One each, unless Clive didn't want his. *'Supper?'* Jack said under his breath. *'For an ant!'*

Supper wasn't the only disappointment, either. Mr Parker was in the kitchen, downing a mug of tea. He wasn't in his black suit tonight but wearing a shirt without a collar and flannel trousers. He said, 'Evenin' Clive,' and, 'Evenin', Wendy,' as they came in; but he just stared at Jack, and at his ear.

'Going out, Mr Parker?' Clive asked him.

'I shall whet my whistle in the "Oak". Just a small Fremlin's Ale.' His voice was less put-on in the kitchen, a bit cockney, and he made a noise, breathing.

'Sounds as if you need something to open up your throat,' Florrie said.

'Asthma's bad tonight.'

''Long as you come back with the same number of legs you take out with you.'

Jack wasn't sure where Mr Parker had his room,

it didn't seem to be in this building, like Florrie's; although at the side of the house he'd noticed a brick stable without any horses, where the colonel's car was parked. It had an outside staircase leading up to a room with a small window.

'Done your blackout, 'fore you go?' Florrie asked Mr Parker.

'Sure have. They're not shootin' me for a spy.'

Jack's eyes opened wide. Was that what they did if you showed a light? Well, he'd make sure he pulled his curtain all the way across tonight.

To his disappointment, Clive did want his biscuit. Mr Parker went out – didn't wash his mug, just plonked it on the table in front of Florrie – and made sure not to include Jack as he said, 'Cheerio.'

Straightaway, Florrie got on with the grown-ups' dinner, and Jack and the others said goodnight and went to bed, taking different directions at the top of the stairs; Clive and Wendy along to doors on the front side of the house, Jack to his room at the back.

He'd better clean his teeth, he thought, before he shut his curtain. His mother had bought him a special tin of tooth powder. He took his brush and face rag along to the bathroom and tried the handle. It wasn't locked, he'd got there first, so he went inside.

'Blimey! Buckingham Palace!'

Everything was shiny – taps, toilet-roll holder, even the lavatory chain – but what really impressed him was the floor. No old lino – this had got to be marble, all big black and white squares like a draughts-board. He took in a long, deep, breath. Living here was like being some sort of a prince, just being able to stretch out his arms without always touching a wall.

He lifted the lavatory seat, which had an extra top on it, pee'd, remembered to pull the chain after, and washed his hands. Looking for somewhere to dry them, he saw a line of towels hanging on hooks on the back of the bathroom door. Above each of the hooks was a small painted sign with a name on it. One said, 'Da', one said, 'Ma', one said, 'Wendy', one said, 'Clive' – and at the end of the line there was an extra hook, with a small gummed-paper label stuck above it. It said, 'Jack'.

He stood staring at it, his chest filling with what seemed like pure oxygen, his head stuffed with pride: until a nagging poked at him, hard. What would his mum think if she could see all this? She wouldn't believe her eyes.

With such a dark curtain at the window, Jack slept longer than usual. It was a rapping at the door that woke him, and the colonel shouting, 'Up and at, 'em, Jack. The sun's burning your eyes out.'

Frightened that the man would come in and throw a jug of cold water over him, Jack yelled, 'Comin'!' and jumped out of bed. He was just pulling on his underpants when a hand came round the door dangling a dressing gown.

'You'll need this, old chap. Wouldn't want to shock the gels …'

'Ta.'

Jack put it on. It fitted quite well, it must have been an old one of Clive's.

The bathroom was empty, except for some steam – they'd beaten him to it this morning – but the steam was luxury, too. It meant he could wash in hot water, and not at a cold tap in the kitchen. There was no luxury about the breakfast, though. Jack's mum usually put more than this in front of him on a Saturday morning. Florrie dolloped a ladle of porridge – burnt sticky, more like glue – and gave him a couple of slices of marmite toast from last night's loaf.

'Any more?' Jack asked. 'Please.'

'Not 'less you're a baker, Jack-me-lad. Didn't know about you, did I, weren't told when I done the shopping.' Florrie stared at him, folded her arms. 'Mi'lady's whimsy.'

And that had Clive snorting porridge up his nose, and choking – which blooming well served him right.

Mr Parker and the colonel had gone off in the Austin before Jack came down for breakfast: and the place felt different. Clive seemed to sit taller; Wendy said dafter things; and Florrie stood about with her arms folded a lot more.

'Now – we're going to show Mardenhurst to Jack,' Lady Ashwell told them all – as Clive washed the breakfast things, Jack dried, and Wendy put things away.

'The village! There's nothing to see,' Clive moaned.

Jack nodded at that. One street! He'd rather play games in the garden.

But Lady Ashwell shook her head. 'Nonsense! There's the church with the finest brasses in this part of the world, the site where the Zeppelin came down, and a superb view over the weald to the South Downs.'

All of which left Jack standing with his left

shoulder down by his knee. Saturday morning in Woolwich was a nip through the market, filching an apple off the greengrocery stall while Old Harry was busy tipping his scales, a ride across the river on the free ferry, and a run back through the foot tunnel shouting rude echoes all the way. Against which – the village church!? And he'd only want to see an old airship crash if there was a skeleton sticking up out of the ground.

'Farmer Hunden's bull!' Clive suddenly splashed his hands into the sink. He'd changed his mind. 'We could show him Hunden's bull.'

'It's certainly a prize creature,' Lady Ashwell said. 'Pride of Hunden's Farm.'

Well, Jack wouldn't mind seeing that. But wasn't Hunden's Farm where Shirley had gone with Rodney Bennett and 'Bully' Betts? The farmer's name had stuck with him, because it had 'Hun' in it, which also meant 'German', didn't it? Not that he wanted to see whiney Shirley, thanks. He was well off here, not being anywhere near Shirley Filer. But a bull that made Clive splash suds up the wall could be well worth a look.

He made sure he left his room tidy. He covered his bed, and put on yesterday's clothes. He'd had a wash, dried his neck on his new towel, cleaned his teeth, and left the bedroom door open to show what a good boy he'd been.

He'd meant that for the lady – he still couldn't get used to thinking about her as Auntie Sylvia – but it was Florrie who appeared in the doorway with her arms folded.

'Where's your dirty pants, then?' She came in and started opening his drawers.

''Aven't got any.'

'You ain't *wearin'* 'em, are you?'

He was – but they weren't dirty, he'd had a good look.

'Off!' she said. She found his other pair, and threw them at him. And she stayed there, staring. Jack stared back. He wasn't going to take his trousers down while this woman was watching. 'Get on with it. I've seen every dingly and dangly a boy's got. If you was to shock me it'd be in the Sunday paper.'

She wouldn't budge. Jack had to do as he was told; and when she took the first pair of pants off him, she held them between her fingers at arms' length as if the state of them could knock her out. 'In this household, pants are one-day items,' she said. 'Leave 'em in the corner of this top drawer. Everything else is a Friday job, like mi'lady told you.'

Jack just sniffed. There were times for arguments, and there were times for just sniffing. He only hoped she wasn't going to march down the stairs with his pants on show like the school caretaker with a dead rat.

Chapter Seven

They walked the length of the drive to the War Memorial, Lady Ashwell pointing out trees and plants on either side. Jack didn't bother trying to remember their names. He knew a rose – but there weren't any of those – and he knew conker trees from over the river in North Woolwich Gardens, but there weren't any of those, either. It was all dead boring, the country: just a lot of green, really. He didn't see any rabbits hopping about, he didn't see any foxes being chased, and he didn't see any snakes slithering in the grass. Clive walked along sharpening a stick with his sheath-knife, and Jack wished he'd brought his black jack-knife with him in case he came across a German paratrooper, but his mother hadn't let him. And Wendy wasn't much fun. She'd moaned about coming, had wanted to paint some scenery for her model theatre; but the lady wouldn't have it.

'It's sunny now, could be our last day of summer peace for some time, and we're going to enjoy it together.'

Enjoy! If this was enjoying, dropping a stink bomb in the Co-op was like top fun at the fair. But Clive was allowed to lead them along a winding lane to the bull. And that opened Jack's eyes. It was in a field that ran down to Hunden's Farm buildings, all on its own, kept away from a herd of cows by a strong wire fence. And it was big! Jack's skin had tingled passing the cows, which were big enough, but as the four of them came to the gate of the bull's field, the creature on the far side started to trot towards them, getting bigger as it came nearer and nearer, going from a cow to a bull to a monster. It didn't come at them like a horse – Jack knew horses, from Woolwich coalmen's dirty nags to great drays from Beasley's Brewery, but they all clopped. This thing came across the grass like a loco. Jack needed a great burst of bravery not to take a step backwards. His heart pumped, and he breathed in hard through his nose so as not to let his mouth drop open. Clive was at the gate, almost leaning over it – and Jack knew that Wendy was looking at him, the London kid, to see what he was going to do. Was he scared? Or was he as brave as her country brother?

The bull looked as if it might come crashing straight through the gate, but it stopped, and tossed its head, the ring through its nose dripping with snot. It snorted, a sudden, deep noise, and it clumped at the hard ground in the gateway with its front hooves. It was taller than the height of the gate, and a marvel to Jack that it stayed on its own side. Scariest of all was its eye on the near side of its head, where the thing had turned sideways on.

'He's accepted us,' Clive said. 'If they're going to charge they keep front on, so their enemy doesn't know their size.'

That was good enough for Jack. He took his next step – forward towards the gate, where he did more than lean over it next to Clive, he sat himself up on the top. He was Jack Bell. 'Moo!' he said to the huge eye.

'Hold tight! Don't fall off! He gave Hunden's man a nasty goring when he got too familiar.'

'He don't scare me. You 'ave to let 'em know who's the guv'nor.' It worked with the coal-yard horses. But there wasn't much more Jack was prepared to do to show off, so he took an interest in the animal's body. It had hardly any horns, which were in front of a big hump and huge sides; but underneath, its dicky wasn't near the back next to the rest of its privates but in the middle of its body, which somehow didn't seem the right place. And it was those other bits that kept Jack staring. Talk about big! They hung there like heavyweight boxing gloves.

'"Herefords",' Lady Ashwell said. 'They're called "Herefords".'

Well, that was a new name, Jack thought. He knew lots of other things to call them, but 'Herefords' had to be the polite word.

'White head and under-belly, otherwise a brownish-red hide, that's your Hereford.'

Ah. She was talking about the whole bull. 'Yeah,' Jack said, as if he'd understood from the start. 'So, has he got a name hisself? Like "Barney" or "Buttercup", or something?'

'Everyone calls him "Charlie",' Wendy said.

'After the man who used to run the "Oak",' Clive put in. 'Don't know why.'

'Nice Charlie,' Jack said, stretching out as if to pat the bull's back but stopping short.

Wendy turned her back on the bull – and on Jack sitting on the gate – and put her head on one side to ask her mother, 'What was it you said about it could be the last day of peace? The actual last *day*?'

'Da was called back to his unit early,' Lady Ashwell said, looking around as if someone else might be listening. 'The word is – and this isn't top secret – that the Prime Minister's going to tell us tomorrow whether or not Herr Hitler has done what we have asked …'

'What's that?' Wendy wanted to know.

'That he should leave Poland alone.'

Jack sniggered. In his house, Po-land was the place where the pot was kept, under the bed.

'It's not funny, Jack. It's very serious. Hitler bombed Poland yesterday. If by eleven o'clock tomorrow morning he doesn't say that won't happen again, we will declare war on Germany.'

Well as far as Jack was concerned they *were* in a war with Germany. His mother was doing overtime making bombs, he was evacuated, and last night everyone had had to put up their blackout. It seemed to him like there was a war.

Slowly, Charlie the bull moved off to a shadier part of his field. And as Jack watched him go, something else caught his eye. Or, someone. Down in the valley at Hunden's farm a couple of people had come out of a door. One of them – he could see her clearly from here – was Shirley Filer. But she looked different. She wasn't wearing her usual raggedy dress but was in a long fawn coat like a milkman's or a grocer's, and gumboots, and she was carrying two buckets. The other person looked like the farmer's wife – who gave Shirley a push to hurry her up.

'I know her,' Jack said, before he could stop himself. 'The one on the left. Goes to our school.' He didn't want to tell these people that she lived upstairs from him in Woolwich in case they asked her to come to tea.

'Milking time,' Lady Ashwell said. 'She's helping with the milking.'

'Squirt, squirt,' said Jack.

'Hunden's got two herds. Friesian dairy cows, over on the other side of the Marden, and Herefords for meat.'

'Da says he's got his bread buttered on both sides,' Clive said.

Lady Ashwell gave him a look. 'We don't repeat Da's observations, Clive. In the village, around the manor, nor …'

'… Even in the open air.'

'And there's no need to be impertinent.'

But Jack wasn't paying too much attention. He was still looking at Shirley, who was being pushed by the farmer's wife into another doorway. *She was working down there.* Those buckets looked heavy, and Shirley had been bent over like Old Mother Cratchett at number three.

The others had started walking back the way they'd come. He turned away and took a flying leap off the gate to catch up with them – landing, as usual, on his feet.

They didn't have to go to church on the Sunday. It was a very different day all round. Everyone went about as if someone was ill and there mustn't be too much noise. Lady Ashwell checked that the wireless in the living room was warmed up and properly tuned to the Home Service, and two chairs were set by it for her and for Florrie. Early on, Jack and the others were told that they need not put on their church clothes, but 'Sunday afternoon respectable' – which didn't make too much difference to Jack until

Florrie brought him a viyella shirt of Clive's, and a pair of longish khaki shorts to be held up by – and here Jack's eyes opened – a snake-clasp belt. His own belt was the buckle sort, frayed leather and coming apart; this was an elastic yellow and green striped belt with which could be made to fit him without having to bore any holes.

'Ta.'

He made no bones about changing, and went downstairs feeling like someone different.

'Spiffo! You do look the part!' Clive said.

'What part?'

'Jolly old holiday.' He pulled a face. 'Except it's village school tomorrow. Mine's closed, so I'm coming with you.'

Jack shrugged. Like most things, he'd face school when he got to it. He was only here while he liked it, wasn't he? If he didn't fancy school, he'd soon work his way back to Woolwich.

Lady Ashwell called the children together in the hallway.

'Florrie and I will be listening to the Prime Minister in the sitting room,' she told them. 'You may play inside, Sunday games, it's still the Sabbath whatever the world is doing, so there's to be no charging around, no outside voices, but toy soldiers, or Dinky cars, model theatre, board games, music practice, or reading ...'

'Books out under a tree?' Wendy asked.

'Books indoors. Sundays are not brown skin days. Remember where we should be at eleven o'clock ...'

Where Jack was dead pleased they wouldn't be, in a boring old church!

'... So you two Ashwells can share your things with Jack. Now off you go – and from eleven o'clock the living room is out of bounds.'

Just then Florrie came down the stairs with a breakfast tray.

'I'm all of a dib-dab, ma'am,' she said. 'Brother Fred's in the navy, and Cousin Cyril's in the Exeter Fire Brigade.' She balanced the tray with one hand and put the other to her mouth as if it was holding back a great wail. 'It's too soon!' she said, shaking her head.

'It's at a quarter past eleven,' Lady Ashwell told her.

'Not the wireless. It's too soon after the last lot, ma'am. To be at war again.'

Everything seemed to go quiet at that, and Jack heard something he hadn't noticed before: the low, slow, tick of the grandfather clock at the foot of the stairs.

'Well, we may not *be* at war. And please don't frighten the children. Mr Hitler may have come to his senses.' Lady Ashwell clapped her hands for everyone to get on with something else.

'Right!' said Jack. 'What shall we have a game at?' He looked at Clive. 'What about "Germans an' English"?'

Lady Ashwell waved her arms in horror. 'Only on paper!' She walked away. 'Tea, Florrie!' she said. 'With a little drop of something in it!'

Wendy went off somewhere else, but Clive winked at Jack and took him back upstairs. 'My room,' he said. 'Fun in my room.'

Jack stayed close on his heels. Clive's room! There'd be some good stuff to play with in there.

The room was much bigger than Jack's and looked out over the front lawn, with a glimpse of the War Memorial in the distance. But the first things he saw were up on the ceiling, hanging by black threads: a silver airliner, two old-fashioned biplanes, and a balloon airship. On the back of the door was a ring-board with five black rings, and beside the wardrobe there was a waste paper basket with a couple of golf putters and some balls in it. And all along the windowsill marched a Grenadier Guards' band of toy soldiers – every instrument Jack could think of. Not that he knew their actual names.

'I collect those,' Clive told him. 'They sell them in the village shop. And the truly good thing is, you can never have doubles; you just have a bigger band.'

Jack blew a raspberry, which was meant to stand for a trumpet. These were a lot different from the soldiers in his biscuit tin at home. None of their paint was chipped, they'd all got their heads, and they all stood straight on their little foot-stands, no leaning sideways or forwards. There wasn't one he'd have to execute, which he sometimes did: leant it up against a piece of coal in the fire and watched it melt into a little dollop of lead.

But they didn't play with the band. Clive took a chair over to his wardrobe, climbed on it, and from the top he lifted down a violin case.

'Do you play?' he asked.

'Not what you've got in there.'

The violin was dusty white on top with some sort of powder, and it had a bow that Clive wound up at one end until it could have been used for firing an arrow. He plucked at the strings and turned the black pegs at the narrow end, then tucked the violin under his chin and played a slow tune.

'"Barcarolle" from *Tales of Hoffmann*,' he said.

'Not "Sausage Roll"?'

Clive snorted and stopped, as if that had been the funniest joke in the world.

'I can play something,' Jack said, before Clive could start again. He looked around – but he knew that what he wanted wouldn't be up here. 'Got any spoons?'

'Spoons?'

'Spoons. What you eat with. Afters' spoons.'

'They're not an instrument. You can't play spoons!'

'I can.'

'Can you? Then I'll get some.' Clive put the violin back into its case, shut it securely, and ran downstairs.

And although he'd left the door open, it gave Jack the chance he'd been wanting – to have a quick look around in Clive's room.

Chapter Eight

Under the bed was the first place. That was where most private stuff was kept in Jack's house. Under his own bed was his tin of toys and a pile of Dandys and Beanos. And he knew all about the Christmas bottles under his mother's bed, and the shoe box of boring photographs, all cardboard pictures of people sitting in front of pots and plants, looking like stuffed dummies.

But under Clive's bed there was nothing but floorboards, not even any dust. The chair was still over by the wardrobe, though, so after a quick look along the landing Jack was up there, and groping. And was this? His fingers could feel the corners of a box, about a ruler and a half long on one side, and a bit shorter on the other. Could it be what he hoped it was? *A train set?* He'd never had a proper train set, only a wind-up baby thing with a giraffe as the engine driver, not one with a transformer and a Flying Scotsman. From that first night in this house, he'd lain in bed and wondered if Clive had a train set, where you could have signals, and points, and send trains down sidings, like trucks in the coal yard.

'Jack! What are you doing up there?'

Jack didn't hesitate. 'Gettin' ready for you to put it back. Give it.' He clicked his fingers. 'The thing you was playing.'

'The violin?'

'That's the bloke. I've found a space.'

'You don't want to hear any more?'

'Not old "Sausage Roll".' Jack looked down at him, eyes into eyes. 'Do you? You said *fun.*'

'I still want to see what you do with these.' Clive took two dessert spoons from his back pocket and waved them at Jack. He handed up his violin case. Jack came down and took the spoons, sat on the chair, and pointed to the bed for Clive to sit upon and listen. He raised his left knee by tucking-in his ankle and lifting his heel. Turning the spoons opposite ways, backs of bowls against one another, he pushed their handles between different fingers of his left hand, tapped the bowls together – not such a tinny sound as the spoons at home – and he started hitting them against his leg and his right hand, which was hovering above.

'I say! Percussion.'

Jack practised a few hits, worked up a fast rhythm, and to the metallic beat he started to sing.

'"Last Sunday Uncle Charlie
Wot lives in Camberwell,
Came to see the trouble an' me,
Watch an' fob on his Derby Kell;
'Cor blimey,' said the missus,
'E can't 'alf do it fly' –
As he upped his tile an' what fell out
But a nice hot chitt'ling pie!"'

He played a flashy riff on the spoons, running them down his splayed fingers, and finishing with:

'"Diddle-diddle dah-dah,
Diddle-diddle dah-dah,
'Ow's your father? All right!"'

'Spiffo! I say! Wow! That's clever.' Clive clapped hard.

'Them's your spoons!' Jack waved them in the air.

'And jolly good, too.' Clive frowned. 'But what language was that you were singing? It was sort of English, but then it wasn't – was it? I didn't know some of those words.'

'They're your Cockney, aren't they?'

'What did they say?'

Jack showed off for a few moments more with the spoons, playing them not only on his left leg and his right hand but up his left arm, on his cheek, the tip of his nose, and his front teeth – which he quickly stopped because these spoons were heavier than he was used to. 'Right – ' he said. 'I'll tell you. You've got *"Uncle Charlie"* an' *"Camberwell"*.'

'Which is a place.'

'*"Came to see the trouble an' me"* – "trouble an' strife" – that's "wife". It's a rhyme, get it?'

'Ah. Yes. Parker says some of those. He says "Barnet Fair" when he means "hair".'

Jack closed his eyes, but only because he couldn't close his ears; he didn't want to hear about flick-your-ear Parker. '*"Watch an' fob"*,' he went on, 'you know them: *"on his Derby Kell"* – "Derby Kelly" – "belly".' Jack patted his own. 'Some person – or it could've been an 'orse.'

'I get it! It sort of makes sense. Go on.' Clive's eyes were wide open.

'*"He can't 'alf do it fly"* – "fly", that's like, "clever". *"Then 'e ups his tile"* – doffs his hat – an' up under there he's hid a chitt'ling pie. Pilfed it off the butcher an' don't want to get caught walking it down the street.'

'Well I never! It's better than learning French.'

Clive reached for the spoons. 'But can I have a go? I won't know the words …'

''Course you can. But it ain't easy.'

Jack swapped places with Clive, the chair being the right height for playing the spoons. He showed Clive how to hold them in the fingers of his left hand, and how to have them loose enough to hit bowl against bowl, then against his leg.

'Right you are, then. Sing suthink an' bash away …'

Clive sat there and had a think. Like Jack, he gave himself a little introduction with the spoons, not so flowing, not so skilled, but with a definite rhythm.

'"God save our gracious King,
Long live our noble King –"'

'You can't do that,' Jack cut in. 'You're s'posed to stand up for that, and you've got to stay sittin' down.'

'Oh, yes.' Clive had another think; went over to the door, closed it, and started again.

'"Auntie Mary had a canary
Up the leg of her drawers,
When she trumped,
Down it jumped,
And flew off out the door …"'

'Oi!' Jack shouted with the shock of it. Old Clive had just sung a rude song! He fell forwards off the bed and lay on the floor laughing, while Clive threw the spoons in the air and dived down next to him – both of them choking and kicking. Gradually they calmed, rolled aside and looked at one another.

'Blimey, Jack!' said Clive.

'Spiffo, Clive!' said Jack.

And that's where they were when they heard the real sounds of God Save the King coming from the wireless downstairs. It was just after a quarter past eleven.

'Britain is at war with Germany,' Lady Ashwell told them, coming into the room. 'I think you should get up off the floor.'

They got up. Clive stood to attention and saluted, just like a soldier. Jack did the same, standing next to him the way he toed the line in the school hall.

'You must be very good now,' Lady Ashwell told them. 'I shall be doing more for the Women's Voluntary Service, so there'll be extra pressure on Florrie …'

The bounce of a dropped pot came from the kitchen. But it was the next thing Jack heard that started his heart thumping. Across the grounds of Ashwell Hall came the seasickness sound of an air raid siren. It growled, wound itself up, then rose and fell, turning Jack's stomach over – like going high past the 'bumps' on the 'plank' in the swing-yard – scary and exciting at the same time.

'Wendy!' Lady Ashwell shouted. 'Cellar!' And, 'Gas masks!' She hurried off along the landing.

Clive's gas mask was hanging on the back of his door beneath the ringboard. Jack wasn't sure where his was, but he ran to look for it. Wendy and Lady Ashwell met him as he got to his room. He pointed up above his head. 'Watch out for parachutes!'

'Cellar, everyone!' Lady Ashwell called out.

She and Wendy went downstairs, while Jack found his gas mask case in the third drawer he tried. He followed them, to where Florrie was standing in the hallway, her gas mask already on.

'Phhph phmmph phmmphy phmmph.' Her voice sounded like an elephant's. She ripped off the mask. 'Phew! Suffocation!'

'Not if properly donned!' Lady Ashwell led them through the kitchen to the cellar entrance, just inside the outer scullery door, where she saw them down and shut the top door behind her. 'Mr Parker prefers to be independent.' The cellar had an electric light, but the first thing she did when they were in there was put a match to a paraffin lantern. 'Just in case.'

Jack looked around. This wasn't like any cellar he'd been in before. There were rows of bottles on their sides in racks, and shelves with jars and boxes on them, some marked in stencil: 'DAY 1', 'DAY 2', 'DAY 3' – up to 'DAY 7'. There were a couple of bottles of whisky and some ginger beers on a shelf, and camp beds standing folded against the wall where a high window had bars inside the black-painted glass.

Lady Ashwell closed the cellar door, pulled a blanket across it, and stuffed a rolled-up mat into the small gap at its foot. 'Da's done well,' she said. '"The Refuge Room".'

Jack followed Florrie's eyes, looking at the ceiling. There was a beam going across the cellar, with a white painted tree trunk propping it in the middle. 'Lor', didn't Parker swear, walking that up from Hunden's farm!'

'Not in front of the children, I hope.'

Florrie sniffed. 'He's one man to the colonel and yourself ma'am, and another to the rest of us …'

Well, Jack would go along with that.

Now no one seemed to know what to say, or to do. All their gas mask cases were open but no one put them on. In practices at school Jack had hated the smell of the rubber, and the horrible way the sides of the mask sucked against his cheeks when he breathed in. He'd definitely wait for the gas warning rattle before he put this on. He cocked his head on one side. With the rest, he stood still, and listened. Could he hear aeroplanes? Could he hear bombs dropping? Could he hear machine guns shooting at German paratroopers coming down out of the sky?

'They've closed all the pictures and theatres,' Florrie said, out of nowhere.

Jack looked at Clive, to see if he was listening for Germans, like him. But the look on Clive's face was very different, as if something was hurting him. Was he dead scared? Had he hit the spoons too hard on his leg?

'Ma – ' Clive said, in a quiet voice. 'Where do we ...?' He started hopping from one foot to the other.

'In the coke hole.' Lady Ashwell went to the far end of the cellar and opened a curtain that was strung across a low doorway. Inside was what looked to Jack like a posh wooden armchair. 'There's a commode, and a bucket. Commode for ladies, bucket for gentlemen. Tinkles only, unless it's an emergency.'

Clive hurried across the cellar and went behind the curtain.

'La-la-la-la-la-la ...' Wendy sang. 'Tinkle, tinkle, little star ...'

'"Auntie Mary la-la-la",' Jack joined in.

'And hand washing in the usual place,' Lady Ashwell called. There was a large sink in the corner.

'It's drinking water, so we're perfectly comfortable down here until – '

'Glory be!' Florrie had the best ears in the place because she seemed to be the first to hear it – that winding-up growl again from over in the village, and then the long, steady, whine of the 'All Clear'.

'The "All Clear". "Raiders passed",' Lady Ashwell said. 'Although I expect it was the Prime Minister giving the country a practice. But it could be real next time, so keep your gas masks handy. And, bucket, Clive, for emptying. There are no fairies.'

They went back upstairs, where to Jack nothing seemed to be at all different from before.

Except, he knew that it was. He was in a real war now.

They still had a Sunday dinner. For this they ate together in the dining room – Lady Ashwell and the children – served by Florrie wearing a starched apron. Jack's mother always cooked a good Sunday dinner, it was the one meal of the week when Jack wasn't itching to get down from the table. But at home there were just the two of them, eating in the kitchen with one swing around with the plates from the gas stove to the table. Here at Ashwell Hall there was an empty chair for the colonel at one end of the dining table, with Lady Ashwell sitting at the other end. Wendy and Clive were one on each side, with Clive moved along a bit to make room for Jack. They had special napkins and rings in here, and the knives and forks were heavy; and instead of Jack's dinner being put in front of him all dished up, there were only a couple of slices of meat on his plate, and he had to help himself to potatoes, greens, and peas from three dishes that Florrie had put down the middle of the table. Watching his p's and q's, he waited for Lady Ashwell to serve herself, then Wendy, then in he went for a good helping of roast potatoes and not much of the other two.

'More green vegetable, please, Jack,' he was told. 'For your skin, and to put a light in your eyes.' Well, he never knew cabbage and peas did that. 'And make the most of the roast beef. Now the war's started we shall soon have food rationing, and you'll have a fraction of the meat on your plate today.'

Forget the meat and the greens, Jack couldn't wait to get stuck into those roast potatoes. Holding his cutlery upright he waited for Clive to serve himself.

'And do lay your cutlery down until I begin. Held like this when the time comes – ' Lady Ashwell leant over and put the knife and the fork into his hands the way she would hold them. 'The knife isn't a dagger and it isn't a pen. And the fork is for piercing, not for scooping …' She demonstrated again.

'Right you are.' These spuds were going to be cold by the time he got one into his mouth.

'And the spoons are for holding like this!' Clive suddenly reached across Jack, picked up his dessert spoon, and put it with his own into one hand. He raised his knee level with the edge of the tablecloth and started to play the spoons. '"Last Sunday Uncle Charlie, wot lives in Camberwell …"'

'Clive!' Lady Ashwell smacked her hand on the table.

'Spiffo!' Jack cried, his eyes all lit up, even before he'd eaten a mouthful of greens.

Wendy put her napkin over her face and pretended she wasn't there. And Clive soon wasn't. He was sent to eat his dinner in the kitchen. And Jack ate his in demure silence, like the good-as-gold evacuee from Depot Street that he was.

Chapter Nine

Shirley wasn't in school on the Monday – not that Jack was looking out for her; he was looking out for himself, as usual. Where Wendy went to school he didn't know, but hers hadn't started yet, so she was left behind to do lessons with her mother. But Clive walked to the village – and the two of them lined up in the small hall with the Union Street children.

Everyone was crowded into the school hall: the locals, back after the holidays, and the Union Street children. Miss Buckshoot, the real village teacher, had put a photograph of King George VI and Queen Elizabeth on the table at the front. The Infants' teacher, Mrs Fossdyke, was at the piano.

'Everyone stand,' Miss Buckshoot commanded.

Everyone stood, including Mrs Rosewarn and the other London teacher, Miss Babcombe.

'To attention.'

They all stood to attention.

'Children, you will know from the wireless and what your parents will have told you that we are now on a war footing with Germany ...'

Jack didn't understand what feet had to do with it, but he knew what she meant.

'We pray for a swift resolution. But today we shall show our patriotism by singing the National Anthem.'

Jack joined in with Clive and the others, giving it everything he'd got. Some of the children who were cubs, scouts, brownies, guides, and church brigade stood and saluted, the way they did on Empire Day – so Jack saluted, too, but like a soldier. And as he stood there to attention, singing and saluting, his chest filled up with pride and his head felt light. He was an Englishman, and he was ready to fight and die for his king and his country.

'All sit.'

It was a shame that was over. Jack looked around him, nodded and winked at some Union Street boys, and pulled faces at the village kids who turned and stared at him.

Mrs Rosewarn looked crabbier than ever, which Jack thought was because the teacher from the village school seemed to be the one in charge. Now Miss Buckshoot told everyone to sit cross-legged and in silence while she sent people were to different rooms. The younger ones went off to the Babies' Room with Mrs Fossdyke, and some of the older village infants came back.

'You are moved up to Class One,' the teacher said.

A couple of older Class Ones came in to join Class Two with Miss Babcombe, and some of the Union Street children were taken off in their place. This left about thirty in the hall.

'Desks are being brought from County Hall,' Miss Buckshoot announced, ' so we shall make do as best we can; and our hall will become Class Three under Mrs Rosewarn.'

Mrs Rosewarn glared along the lines.

'Rats' tails!' Jack's mouth slid to Clive.

'Talking!'

Clive kept his mouth shut.

'The furniture is expected forthwith.' Miss Buckshoot stood and pointed at the children, every row. 'Until such a time as it arrives, your seat will be the floor, and your desktop will be ... the floor.' She turned to Mrs Rosewarn. 'Did you bring your pencils and exercise books?'

The look on Mrs Rosewarn's face put Jack in mind of his mother's when he'd left the milk in the sun.

'We came from bomb-threatened London with what we stood up in,' Mrs Rosewarn said. 'On government instructions.'

Miss Buckshoot nodded. 'Those same instructions that we have obeyed at our end. But you shall share our stock for now, and kindly post requisitions to your council as soon as possible.' She smiled at Mrs Rosewarn, whose face said that someone was going to catch the rough end of this ticking off.

And it had to be poor old Clive who copped it.

He had brought a letter with him, from his mother. Jack knew what was in it because they'd read it as they walked to school. Because it was a 'BY HAND' letter the envelope wasn't stuck down.

It was in small curly writing that Jack couldn't quite make out, so Clive read it aloud.

'*Dear Miss Buckshoot,*

As Chairwoman of the School Managers I wish you every success with the integration of the London children with our local boys and girls. I hope that everybody rises to the occasion with patience and good behaviour ...'

Jack listened for a word or two about how patient and good he'd been, but there was none.

'*... The bearer of this letter is my son Clive, whom you will remember was with with you until Standard One,* *when we removed him to St Wilfred's Boys' School in Headcorn. St Wilfred's has decided to close its doors for the duration, therefore I wish to re-enrol Clive at Mardenhurst.*

To clarify matters, I shall place a copy of this letter in the Minutes of the next Managers' meeting.

Yours sincerely,
Sylvia Ashwell.'

Miss Buckshoot had gone out of the hall with the new Class Two. 'Monitors will bring your stationery supplies,' she said to Mrs Rosewarn as she went, leaving her with the new Class Three, the Woolwich and the Mardenhurst children still sitting in separate lines. Mrs Rosewarn called the Union Street register first, noting that Bennett, Betts, and Shirley Filer were absent.

Jack put up his hand. 'Shirley Filer's milking cows,' he told her.

'Being a sight more useful than a Jack Bell, then.' Now she spotted Clive, sitting among the Union Street children. She marched along the line and stood over him. 'You're not a Union Street boy,' she said. 'Shouldn't you be over there for your register?'

Clive stood up.

'Sit down.'

Clive sat down, but offered up his letter.

Mrs Rosewarn waved it away as if it were a pesky wasp. 'I don't want a letter from your mother at this juncture. Go and sit over there.'

Clive got up again and walked to a line of village children, who knew him.

'Wotcha,' he said, sounding a bit like Jack. He did a mock bow and said, 'I'm not here and I'm not there, but shuffle up, chaps.'

'How dare you saunter over there and converse?'
Mrs Rosewarn was over at him before he could sit
himself down. As she went, she rolled the black-
covered register into something looking like a
policeman's truncheon and whacked him round the
head with it. Hard. Twice. Left side and right side.
Clive staggered, and fell back.

'That wasn't fair!' he said, a hand on each ear.

'You want another?'

And at that moment Jack felt something he'd
never felt before. Anger for someone else. A taste
in his mouth that made him want to run across the
hall and slosh Mrs Rosewarn. She'd really hurt old
Clive. The cowardly old cow! But what troubled
him more was that he sat still, did nothing; and
had to wait until playtime to put his arm around
his new mate.

'I'm all right,' Clive said, shrugging him off. 'I'm
not a cissy.'

''Course you ain't.'

'I can box. Da's taught me.' He took up a pugilist
stance like an old-fashioned ring fighter.

'What's that?'

'Boxing.'

Jack shook his head. 'Forget boxing. It's *fighting*
what counts.' He took up the same boxers' stance, the
two of them facing one another as if they were in the
Albert Hall. Clive moved his feet to come dancing in
towards Jack, but before he could get within reach,
Jack suddenly took a scissors kick at Clive's leading
arm and knocked it into the air, following up at speed
with a grab round Clive's neck and a quick wrestle
to the ground.

'I say …!'

'See?' Jack got off Clive and pulled him to his feet. 'That's how you win 'em.'

'Gosh.'

'Bit of a surprise.'

Clive smiled, and shook Jack's hand warmly. 'Spiffo – so we're the Two Musketeers! We could take on anyone.'

'Yeah.' Jack wasn't up with these Musketeers, but he knew what Clive meant.

'"All for one, and one for all".'

'That's about the size of it.'

Clive pulled an eager face. 'Just think what we can do to a German spy if we catch one.'

'Yeah!' Jack tasted the spit in his mouth. 'Spiffo! The Hun won't know he's born, will he?'

Clive wouldn't let Jack say anything back at home about what had happened. Jack understood. You didn't. You got the cane, or a school bully scragged you, but you kept them to yourself: you weren't a tell-tale-tit. Clive had picked himself up and taken his letter to Miss Buckshoot at dinner time, and Clive's name was read out by Mrs Rosewarn from the new register, at the end of the girls.

There was plenty going on at Ashwell Hall that evening, anyway. Mr Parker had been to fetch the colonel and brought him back in the Austin 10 with its pennant fluttering.

'Don't go far to his regiment, does he?' Jack said to Clive, both up a tree and sharing a branch.

'Can you keep a secret?'

'Didn't tell about your whacking, did I?'

'He's only down at Dover. Have you heard of Dover Castle?'

''Course! Dover Castle.' The real one was a pub along the Plumstead Road.

'Well, that's where he is. He's ...' Clive tapped his forehead. 'Intelligence. Not with a regiment, or anything. "Top Brass". War Office. But, no splitting!'

'On me mother's death bed.'

'It's all down deep, in the White Cliffs, under the castle. Sometimes when's he's got a lot of planning to do next day he comes home for a good night's sleep, out of all the hurly-burly.'

Jack nodded as if he understood, although he'd never had a bad night's sleep in his life.

Now that they were at war the colonel kept out of everybody's way, wasn't the sparky weekend person he'd been on the Friday. Mr Parker poked his nose into the kitchen when Jack was there, but he seemed to be somewhere else in his mind, too, and he left Jack alone; and after the blackout was all in place, Jack, Wendy and Clive went up to bed. It had been a funny old day. School, not a lot different with old Stroker. Spaghetti-on-toast for tea and tree climbing in the garden – not a lot different. Bathroom – tons different from home – and then bed. But no difference like feeling homesick, the way some of the Union Street kids had cried at school. Jack hadn't even thought about his mother after Lady Ashwell had told him that everything was quiet in London. It was just old Clive who'd made things different, getting whacked by Stroker – which still twisted up Jack's insides.

It could have been that twisting that stopped him getting off to sleep; or it could have been that he was still getting used to it being so quiet down here. Woolwich was noisy all the night; their house in Depot Street was near the back of the Empire Theatre music hall, the trams ran along Beresford Street until late, and early mornings had the coal-yard and the market starting up. So this quietness in the country seemed like a sort of noise to Jack. And what he heard that night, he heard quite clearly.

It came from under his window: a scrunch, scrunch, scrunch on the stony path; not like someone walking on it – he'd done it a couple of times and it kicked up a noise – but like someone creeping, being secret. *And the colonel was here in the house, wasn't he?* Going by what Clive had said, he was the sort of 'Top Brass' a German spy could be creeping about looking for …

Jack threw off his top blanket, went to the window, opened his curtains, and looked down. And, yes! There was someone down there! Fright shot a sudden sheet of ice from his feet to his head. There was someone outside, wearing a trilby hat and a raincoat, going off round the corner of the house, bent over as if he was making himself small. Looking just like a spy: just like in the cartoons in the *Daily Mirror*.

Jack didn't know what to do. Sound the siren by shouting? All the house was quiet, he'd heard the grown-ups go to bed – and the colonel was supposed to be getting a good night's sleep for all the planning he'd got to do in the morning. What if he woke him up and it turned out the man in the hat and the raincoat was only Parker sneaking back from the pub?

He found his torch, came out of his bedroom, and tiptoed along to Clive's room. He didn't knock, didn't want Clive shouting to come in. He went inside and shone his torch on Clive's face.

'Uh? Who? Is it an air raid?'

'Sssh.' Jack put his hand across Clive's mouth, which made him struggle, sitting up.

'It's me. Jack.'

'What do you want?'

Quickly, Jack told him; and the reason why he hadn't woken the colonel.

'Yes, could be Parker,' Clive said. 'He smells of beer sometimes if you get too close. But – '

The two of them looked at one another, still by the glow from Jack's torch.

'Could be going out to do a burglary.'

Jack tingled when Clive said the words.

'What?'

'There are lots of big houses around Mardenhurst, with loads of valuable stuff. There've been several burglaries recently. Da thinks someone takes the stuff and sells it in London. And Parker's creepy. He sucks up to Da and Ma but I wouldn't trust him any further than I could throw him.'

'Or – ' and Jack thought about what the man had looked like in his hat and raincoat – not so much like a burglar, as – *'He could be a spy!'*

Clive smacked his own knee. 'Could be, could be! You're right!' His eyes stared into Jack's like someone's who has seen the truth. 'Da's got Parker's work references – but he'd have them, spies are here from years before the war; years before! He says they live like ordinary English people, do ordinary jobs, but when there's a war they're ready to come out behind enemy lines like slithery snakes.'

Jack shivered. This was exactly the sort of thing old 'Stroker' had said. *Had he seen a German spy tonight?*

'He's not been with us for ever.' Clive put on his dressing gown. He went to the side of his wardrobe and lifted his two golf putting sticks from the waste basket. He gave one to Jack. 'Come on,' he said. 'Let's do a reconnaissance.'

'Yeah.' Jack didn't know what one of those was, but it sounded right. He followed Clive out of the bedroom. They headed for the stairs.

'Use the sides,' Clive said. 'Like burglars ourselves. It's the middles of treads that creak.'

One each side, Jack having to hold his putting stick in his left hand, they went down the stairs and stood silently in the hallway. The grandfather clock sounded loud enough to be heard in the village, covering up other sounds and making Jack feel icy again. They listened. What was Clive going to do? Were they going to go outside, to follow where Jack had seen Parker going – if it *was* Parker?

Clive went to the front door. He looked at the lock and the bolts. 'All secure,' he whispered.

'All secure,' Jack whispered back.

Clive tiptoed towards the kitchen. Gripping the door knob, he opened the door fast – a sudden movement that made Jack jump. 'Doors squeak when you open them slowly,' he said. 'So you take 'em by surprise.'

They went into the kitchen. Was this sort of clever stuff why old Clive didn't always eat everything at teatime? Did he creep downstairs in the middle of the night and pilfer from the larder?

Clive went to the very back door, in the porch. Again, he checked the lock and the bolts. 'All secure,' he said, a bit louder this time.

'All secure,' Jack said, still whispering.

'And the windows are all secure …'

'All windows secure.'

'… So no burglar can get in without the devil of a noise.'

Jack took a relaxing breath. Good. They weren't going outside – not with him in his bare feet and his gappy pyjama trousers.

'We'll go back to bed, but lock our doors.'

'Yeah. Lock our doors.' Except, Jack's door didn't have a lock – but he'd push his chair across it and hope he woke up before Florrie came up in the morning.

'And I'll tell you what – '

'What?'

'Tomorrow, after school, we'll rig up a communications system, your room to mine, my room to yours. An alarm. Then we can both be on red alert.'

'Red alert!' Jack shivered, thrilled at the thought of alarms, and a proper plan.

Clive left the kitchen door open, didn't risk a slam, and they went back up the stairs at the sides.

'Can I have a lend of the golf stick?' Jack whispered on the landing, before he went off on his own.

'For the duration,' Clive told him. 'All for one, and one for all.'

And with a salute to each other they went to their bedrooms.

Where Jack lay awake with his golf club, listening through the longest night of his life – just in case the man had been a burglar trying to get in; but wanting it to have been Parker, a slithery snake German spy that he could catch.

Chapter Ten

Shirley came to school on the Tuesday – and did she look rough! Jack reckoned she always did, but today she looked worse than ever. She threw herself down into one of the new desks as if she was worn out. Only one of the Union Street boys at Hunden's farm came with her; Rodney Bennett told Mrs Rosewarn that 'Bully' Betts had been bitten by a dog.

'And where were you yesterday?'

'Busy, Miss. Farmer says boys is excused school when there's War Effort work to do.'

'Does he? And what work would that be?'

'Butchering, Miss.'

'*Killing?*'

'No, Miss. Cutting up bits o' meat.'

'That's "butchery".'

Mrs Rosewarn turned on Shirley, whose head was down on her arms. 'And what's your excuse, Filer?'

'Eva said we had to wash out the milking parlour proper.'

'You call your foster mother "Eva"?'

'No, Miss. Eva's her daughter.' Shirley turned to look along the line of girls' desks and pulled a face.

'Then kindly tell Eva's mother that if you miss school in future – for whatever reason – I shall need a note.' And, to Jack's surprise, she asked Shirley a question that seemed to come from someone else: some kind person.

'Have you been given any breakfast, girl? Or, you, Bennett?'

'Yes, Miss.'

'Five o'clock 's'morning, Miss.'

'Both of you? At five a.m.?'

'Yes, Miss.'

'And what have you been doing since then?'

'Milkin'.'

'Cleaning the chopping blocks, Miss.'

Jack straightened up and felt like a lord. He'd got out of bed when Florrie knocked at half past seven, and eaten his porridge and toast at eight o'clock.

'Well, we all have our duties and errands in life.' Mrs Rosewarn suddenly became old 'Stroker' again. She turned the ruled blackboard around to show the other side, where twenty adding, subtracting, multiplication and division calculations were neatly chalked. 'So, there's a board of sums to get your brains working, all of you. Use your rough work books.' Without leaving her own desk she skimmed new exercise books to Shirley and to Rodney Bennett. 'You can enter your names on the front in ink later. Now, school dinners ...' She set about adding up the dinner numbers while Jack set about his own additions. He was quite good at arithmetic; he sat in the second top division back at Union Street, and it was something he could usually get on with. But he couldn't stop taking sideways looks at Shirley. She was a snivelly misery most of the time, a nose dripper, a dish-rag girl. Her mum was a good laugh, who got on well with his own mum, but he never had any more to do with Shirley than pulling faces at her. The face she was pulling today, though, was more like a firework night mask with pin-holes for eyes and a slit for a mouth. She looked like someone who's just seen a tram run over a man on a bike.

Jack got on. You got on with stuff in school, or you got lines, or the stick. But at playtime in the small yard he pointed her out to Clive.

'See her? Shirley?'

'Hunden's new milkmaid?'

'Yeah. I know her.'

Clive looked at Jack as if he was talking nonsense. 'You would. She's come with your school from London.'

'Yeah, but I know her more than that.' Jack didn't want to give away too much. 'Her mum knows my mum. They both work in the Arsenal, making bombs.'

'Wow! Ker-boom!' Clive imitated a bomb going off.

'She's drippy at home, but she looks different down here. Still drippy, but … different. Like she's ill.'

'Hunden's a pig.' Clive put his hand over his mouth, as if Lady Ashwell might have just heard him. 'That's a beastly thing to say, but it's true. The Hunden's bought Red House Farm when the old farmer died, and they're not the same sort of people. They're rough and ready from somewhere else, and they don't have respect for the animals.'

'Respect?' Jack knew 'respect', it's what Mrs Rosewarn said boys had to give to girls, taking off their caps, and bowing in Country Dance. But, respect for cows and bulls …?

'You have to be an animal's master, but you don't have to be cruel to him.'

'Got you.' Jack couldn't pretend he'd never been

cruel to an animal, so he shut his eyes on that thought, and nodded.

'Treats his workers like skivvies, locals don't stay there long. Ma says the Hundens have got a different set of values from Mardenhurst people. She thinks he might be a bit ... not properly English.'

Well, Jack thought, they had Scots people and Welsh people and Irish people in Woolwich, all sorts came to join the Royal Artillery up at the barracks. Northerners, too. Other than that, there were some Chinese who ran small seamen's shops along Plumstead High Street, and Hunden's voice was a bit as if he'd come over the river from the docks. Some market people were like Mrs Hunden, too, shouty with big muscles, the same as funfair people up at Woolwich Common. Jack bet she could push you about if she wanted to. He'd never in his life felt sorry for soppy Shirley; but, 'Poor old Filer,' he said.

'Anyhow, our secret communication system,' Clive went on. 'I've had a good brain-rattle. Have you?'

'Not 'alf.'

'What did you come up with?'

'All sorts. But you go first.'

'Well, I've got one idea that could be a corker.'

'Yeah?'

Clive was almost dribbling with his idea. He must have had it when he'd finished the board of arithmetic, because he hadn't said anything when they'd walked to school.

'Wendy's bike and my bike have got dynamos on the front wheels for the lamps. You know about dynamos ...?'

''Aven't actually got one.' Jack didn't have a bike to put one on, either.

'You know the little wheel that rubs on the side of the tyre and generates electricity ...?'

'Oh, yeah, that ...'

'Well, Da says with the blackout we can't have lights that bright, which means we can take them off – and you have one and I'll have one. We run a long wire under the carpets from my room to yours, and when I want to alert you I rub my dynamo back and forth along the carpet, as if it were the side of the tyre, and the lamps shines in your face.'

Jack's eyes opened wide: this sounded good.

'And if you want to alert me – you do the rubbing, and the lamp shines on my face.'

''Yeah! Real secret stuff ...'

'Unless you've got a better wheeze ...'

'No. About the same, really. Only – ' Jack was good at picking up on things – and at lying. 'I'd reckoned batteries. But dynamos is good.'

'They're only "on" when you rub them, unlike batteries, which would waste, being on all night.'

'Essactly. But – ' And Jack was suddenly proud of this – 'Fixing up little lights over our heads is gonna be hard; an' I might be turned over the other way. What about if we have them little magnet bells like you rig up in science?' At Union Street the top class had gas taps and burners too; perhaps there was a drawer of bells here. 'Then we can have 'em under our beds.'

'Spiffo! Splendid. Two brains, Jack! Two brains!' Clive knocked on Jack's forehead, as if he was it were a door. It hurt a bit, but Jack felt proud. 'We could have a snoop here – but Da's got all sorts of stuff in the stables, we'll look there first. There are shelves and cupboards of all sorts of useful things.'

'Wire. We'll need a long bit of wire.'

'Insulated.'

''S' right.'

'We'll pace out the run from my room to yours …'

'And my room to your'n …'

'… Add a third for deviations …'

'Take away the first number you thought of …'

'Ha! Then it's, "Bob's your uncle"!'

'An' "Fanny's your aunt".'

Jack stared into Clive's eyes, and Clive stared back. 'The Two Musketeers!'

'Two for one an' one for two!' Jack shouted – when his shoulder was suddenly wrenched around. 'Oi!'

It was Rodney Bennett.

'Bell!'

'Wha'?'

'You sent your postcard home yet?'

'No.' Jack hadn't told Lady Ashwell about the postcard because he wasn't all that good at writing, and he didn't want her to get Clive or Wendy to help him – that would have been all wrong.

'We've 'ad to send ours with 'ow good it is, where we are.'

'Oh, yeah? Even though it ain't?'

'Shirley, an' all.'

'So?

'Well, your mum knows 'er mum.'

'Sort of.' Jack didn't want any more said in front of Clive. 'What about it?'

'You've gotta write your card an' tell your mum

86

to tell 'er mum to come down an' see where we're living ...'

'I'll try.' Jack wasn't Bennett's size, but usually he still wouldn't stand for being told what to do by anyone; being big wasn't everything in a fight. Right now, though, he didn't want this talk to go on much longer; he didn't want Shirley's closeness to him in Depot Street to come out.

'You do it.' Bennett grabbed Jack's shoulder and squeezed it.

'Get off! Said I'd try.' Jack dipped out of the grip and stood up again, his fists at the ready. 'Now clear off!' He saw Clive take a step back. Good old Clive. Clive was making room for a haymaker.

The bell rang just then, and everyone froze. Miss Buckshoot and Mrs Rosewarn were both in the yard.

'Lines,' Miss Buckshoot shouted. 'Girls first.'

Jack gave himself a yard's distance, too. 'That's you, Bennett,' he sneered. And his stomach turned – but not in fear at what he might have started, but at everything that was suddenly going on down here in Mardenhurst.

War was a proper old mix up, wasn't it?

The colonel's car stood gleaming inside the front end of the stable block. The Ashwells kept no horses these days, so all the stalls had been taken out to make a work area at the rear where there were benches and drawers, drills, a lathe, and shelves of oils, and paints, and ironmongery.

Jack and Clive waited until Mr Parker cycled to the village to post Lady Ashwell's letters. His room was right above their heads, and they didn't want him hearing them rooting around down here. But with him wobbling off on his bike – the car was for the colonel and for emergencies – they had about twenty minutes to themselves.

'Whoo!' To Jack this place was like a shop without a shopkeeper. *All the stuff in here!* Opening any drawer, looking in any cupboard, his eyes went dry with staring. There were jam jars of all sizes of nails, screws, and bolts; tobacco tins marked 'drills', and 'bits', and 'washers'; tins, bottles, and cans of paints of all colours; and, in an old wardrobe fitted out with new shelves, the colonel's tools were laid out neatly. A handy bag and Jack could have done a good trade around the stalls at the back end of Woolwich market.

But it was a scruffy drawer marked 'Odds and Ends' at the bottom of an old dresser that had Clive shouting.

'Spiffo!'

'What you got there?'

Clive turned around, his eyes agleam. He was holding up what looked like a couple of thin metal strips, about half an inch wide.

Jack frowned. It wasn't a bell, it was just old metal. He looked for wire – which he knew he'd find somewhere; just about everything useful was here. And he did. Down a brick buttress ran a line of hooks, and hanging on each one was a reel of wire, all different thicknesses, some bare, some covered in brown cord.

'Here's your wire.'

'Good man!' Clive came over and selected a likely reel, running it out and measuring it like a curtain seller. He started at the tip of his nose and took his arm out straight, as far as it would go, the wire running with it. 'One yard,' he said. He did it again. 'Two yards.' And so on, until he'd got the twenty-five yards they'd paced out along the landing. He went to another reel, where the wire was thinner, but covered in black rubber. He pulled off about six inches of this, now holding both wires in one hand. ''Pliers.' He snapped his fingers at Jack. 'Tool cupboard.'

For once Jack didn't mind having fingers snapped at him, not by Clive, not on a secret mission. He scooted across to the old wardrobe and picked a pair of pliers. Clive cut the wire and replaced the reel.

'Keep the pliers.'

Jack put them in his pocket. And heard the sudden squeal of a bicycle brake.

'Blimey!'

'Parker! The "Oak" must've been closed. Get down. Under the car!'

Like a disappearing rodent Jack squeezed himself beneath the Austin's running board and pulled himself in, leaving room for Clive, who ended up facing down. But there was no room for him to turn over, he had to stay like that. Jack stared up at the mud-caked underside of the Austin and breathed in the oily smell of the engine. But Clive had a better view out, like a man on reconnaissance.

Jack – who could see nothing – heard the door to the stable block open.

'He's coming in.'

The footsteps and the sound of wheezy breathing came close. *Please don't drive the car out!* The two of them would get skinned alive if it moved. But the footsteps went on past the car to somewhere over at the back end of the stables.

'Can you see him?' Jack tried to whisper, but it came out louder than he'd wanted.

'Sssh!'

The footsteps came back. *Had he been heard? His stupid growing-up voice didn't always do what he told it.*

But Parker went on, and out of the stable, closing the door behind him.

On Clive's orders they gave it a count of a hundred, and then another hundred, before they came out – oily and flaked with wheel-arch and under-running board mud. Jack wanted to be off. Never stick around when you've been up to no good. But Clive tiptoed to the far end of the stable.

'He came back here. Put something in the cupboard over the sink.'

The sink was more like a square trough, shallow and low, with a polished bucket standing in it. Clive went to the large cupboard on the wall behind, which he opened. Jack could see jars of salts and washing flakes, and brushes. But what Clive fished out was an old, slim exercise book, reddish with swirly lines on the cover.

'I think it was this he put in.' He opened it.

Jack looked over his shoulder. The pages were scruffy, but each was numbered in the corner in pencil, normal numbers, one, two, three, and so on. On the top line of the first page was a line of numbers: *8 11 24 19 21 20 25 11 31*, and under it was another string of numbers on a separate line, looking like a code: *29 21 18 25 11 18 11 31 25 26 24 11 11 26 – 19 7 26 26 14 11 29 25* – just numbers, with a cross against it at the end of the line. The next page had similar patterns of numbers on it, this time with a tick at the end of the lower line, and so did the third and the fourth. In all six or seven pages were written on.

'What's all that?'

Clive shrugged.

But Jack thought he knew. Each page had different numbers at the top and different lines of numbers underneath, with ticks or crosses against them. 'Them's codes,' he said. He took a deep breath. 'Spy codes!'

'Wow!'

'Looks like it, don't it?'

'Spiffo, Jack – you could be dead right!' Quickly, Clive put the book back where he'd found it. 'He's certainly got some secret reason for not wanting this code book found in his room.'

Jack saw a picture in his head of Parker against the wall with his hands up while soldiers turned his room upside down. Sweet!

'Come on, we've got stuff to do …'

Jack wasn't sure what that was; probably get the wire down under the carpet if it was quiet upstairs. But he didn't know about those strips of metal. They wouldn't be any good as bells, he knew that.

And he was even more puzzled when they got indoors. With the strips up his sleeve, Clive went to the glass-fronted bookcase in the sitting room and took out a large book: *Arthur Mee's Children's Encyclopedia*.

'Reading? We gonna do reading? About codes?'

'Later. Something else first. Come on.' And, giving

the encyclopedia to Jack to carry, Clive led the way up the stairs, even faster than his Da had gone with Jack's suitcase.

Whatever they were going to read, this was serious now – because this was about spying, and war, and beating the Germans, whether he and Clive were kids or not.

Chapter Eleven

What they did was look at a picture, which was under 'E' for 'Electricity', although the photograph didn't look anything like a bell to Jack. It showed a strip of metal sticking up in a 'Z' shape and fixed to a board. Coming from the bottom of a curly wire there was another piece of wire touching the top of the metal; and from the bottom of the metal a third wire was connected to a flat torch battery.

'That spiral bit's the coil – with a nail in the middle of it, making an electromagnet.'

'Yeah, thought so.' And, just in time before he needed to ask, Jack read the print under the picture. 'A SIMPLE BUZZER'. 'Spiffo!' he said. 'Just what I was thinkin' …'

'We can soon rig this up. I'll get the dynamos off the bikes, we can wire them up instead of using batteries.'

There was a rattle of Clive's doorknob and in came Wendy.

'Phew!' she stuck out her lower lip and blew a breath up her face, parting her fringe. 'I'd rather go to school than have Ma as my teacher. What are you two lucky ducks doing?' She looked over to where they were kneeling. 'Got your noses stuck in an encyclopedia?'

Jack wanted her to think he was clever enough to be happy doing that. 'Do you do science at your school?' he asked, like a fellow scholar.

'This sort of thing?' Wendy sighed, and sat on

Clive's bed, heavily. 'Not a lot. But I'd rather be there right now. Ma doesn't recognise lesson bells or breaks, she just steams on for hours at a time ...'

'Poor old Wen.'

'And being home all day with Florrie twittering about, and Parker being around in every room like a bad smell – it's stinking and rotten here with you two off at school.'

'We're rigging up a communication system, Clive to Jack, Jack to Clive, room to room.'

'That's exciting.' Wendy sat forward on the bed. 'Can you fix me in on the circuit?'

'Sorry, Wen – it's two-way.'

But she gave permission for her bicycle dynamo to be 'requisitioned', as Clive called it, which he went out to do in the bike shed, while Wendy helped Jack with hiding the wire under the carpets. This first wire would be the test, from Clive's dynamo to Jack's room; if this worked they'd run the second wire later.

The carpets at Ashwell Hall went nearly to the walls, leaving gaps of about six inches of floorboard all around, but Wendy cleverly picked the darkest place under a dresser for the wire to run beneath Clive's carpet, then took it through the door-jam, and back under the carpet on the landing where there was a vase of dried grasses on the floor. It was a straight run after that, crossing the landing and along to Jack's room, outside which was an upright chair where Florrie rested her dirty-washing basket.

'Where would you like it in here?' Wendy asked. 'Your terminal?'

'Under the bed, the same as in Clive's room?'

'Yeah. That's the ticket for soup.'

'You do talk funny, Jack.'

'Do I?' He thought he talked the way people talked, although not posh like Lady Ashwell.

'I do like to hear it. It's different.'

'I'll play you my spoons if you like, and sing you a song with *loads* of funny talk in it ...'

'Will you? Spoons? Percussion, isn't it? That would be splendid.'

'And you must see my Theatre Royal. "Lady Precious Stream".'

'Smashin'.'

Wendy got on with feeding the wire from beneath the carpet and left it under Jack's bed, at the head end. Jack didn't need the pliers for this first run; Clive had measured up to within a foot of what they'd needed. And soon he was in there with them, having inspected what they'd done.

'Jolly fine job,' he said.

'My pleasure to help.' Wendy stood up.

'Hold up!' Jack put a finger to his lips. He could hear a noise outside on the landing and it didn't sound like Clive. It was Parker making those wheezing noises down in his throat, as if he was clearing it to say something. In the bedroom the pair of them stopped and looked at one another.

'Even if he wasn't a spy or a burglar, he's a funny bloke, i'n't he?'

Wendy wrinkled up her nose. 'It used to be Florrie and her husband looking after the house,' she told Jack, keeping her voice down. 'Alfred. We lived in Chelsea, near Da's regiment at the Barracks. Then when Grandpa Hamilton died we all came here.'

'Ah.'

'That was when I was twelve.'

'So you 'aven't been here all that long?'

'Not to live; but we used to come here a lot to see Grandpa.'

Jack shot a look at the door as the knob slowly turned. But it was Clive, dusting his hands together. 'All done. Dynamos are in my room, we'll rig them later.' He looked from one to the other of them. 'You all right?'

'Parker was outside,' Wendy told him. 'I don't like him upstairs in the house. Not like dear old Alfred …'

'We got Parker when he died; but because he and Florrie aren't married, he lives over the stables.'

Jack thought about what the others had said. 'So you 'aven't known Parker all that long, neither?'

'Not really,' Clive put in. 'He said he went to be a soldier but they wouldn't have him because of his chest; so Da took up his references and offered him to be his driver and our handyman. But he's not like Alfred was …'

'A German spy wouldn't be, would he? Underneath?'

'A "sleeper",' Wendy said in a sinister voice. 'That's what they call them. I read it in Da's *Telegraph*.'

'Yeah,' Jack agreed, 'one of them secret people come years ago that old "Stroker" was talking about …' Jack repeated the things Mrs Rosewarn had said about the German spies who'd been planted like trees – before the war by Hitler. 'An' that's a teacher who said that.'

'And we've found his notebook with codes in it …'

'Wouldn't it be spiffing if he was!' Wendy was

almost too loud in her excitement. 'But, boring Parker ...?'

'Oh, they're dashed clever, spies. But he's not a gentleman like Alfred was.' Clive twisted his face about for a moment, as if he was deciding what to say. 'Don't take this the wrong way, Jack – but he's rougher, more *east London* than Alfred and Florrie.'

''S'all right. I'm *south* London, thanks!'

'Of course you are. But you know what I mean – he's *too much*. And you're you. He sort of puts things on. He calls his socks "Tilburys".'

Jack snorted. 'Well, that's wrong for a start. They're "Chathams". "Chatham Docks" – socks.'

'Not "*Tilbury* Docks"?'

'Nope. Never heard it said.'

'Just as if he *is* pretending, then ...' Wendy sat on the bed, her mouth open.

It all fitted to Jack. *Pretending* was right. That was why Parker had flicked his ear. And why he'd given him those rough words. The man was twitchy about a real Londoner coming to live here.

'Whooooer!' he said, as if a ghost had just drifted through the wall. The three of them stared at one another, and Jack electric, as if his dynamo buzzer had just gone off.

The dynamo worked! Before they ran the second wire from Clive's room he tested it using a torch bulb screwed into a holder, borrowed from the footlights of Wendy's model theatre. He attached two stripped wire-ends to the dynamo's terminals, and the other ends to the bulb holder. On his hands and knees he gripped the dynamo and spun its knurled wheel backwards and forwards across the carpet; the same as if the wheel had been rubbing against the side of a bicycle tyre. And the bulb lit up.

'Spiffo!'

'You're a clever ol' cock!'

'Splendid!' Wendy joined in.

Clive put on a successful inventor's look. 'I'll make the buzzers in the bike shed,' he said, as serious as the colonel planning something at Dover Castle.

'Can we help?' Wendy asked.

'I'm best solo, it's a jolly small shed. You run the second wire. Take these …' Clive got up and reached into a drawer, pulling out a small bag that clinked and chinked. 'If anyone comes you can pretend you're playing marbles along the landing.'

'Alleys!' Jack said. But when he tipped them onto his palm he saw that these weren't the green alleys used as washers in the tops of bottles, but bright, swirly, 'rainbows'.

'That's a wizard idea, Clive,' Wendy said. 'You could be a spy yourself.'

Clive just shrugged. Jack suddenly knelt, picked up the dynamo, and ran it hard across the carpet, twice as fast as Clive had done – which blew the little bulb.

'That won't happen with a buzzer,' Clive said. 'Sorry, Wen.'

'It's all right. I've got some spares.'

Jack said nothing, but felt a bit better about Wendy not saying he'd make a good spy, too. He'd show them, though. He'd show them.

Chapter Twelve

Shirley looked even worse the next day. 'Bully' Betts was back, not looking any different from before, and Rodney Bennett came into the playground looking around him with a scowl – but somehow not spotting where Jack and Clive were standing, over by the boys' lavatories.

Jack left Clive and sidled along to Shirley, who was drinking from the metal cup at the water fountain. As she bent to drink at the end of the short chain he saw the back of her neck. It was red raw with fingernail marks. He didn't like the soppy, stupid, girl – but she did come from Woolwich, and she did live upstairs from him.

'You been scragged by Betts and Bennett?'

'No!'

'Who done it, then? Someone's 'ad a good go at your neck.'

'No one's done nothing.'

'No – don' look like it, neither.' Jack was in the open playground now – Clive, too – and Bennett had seen them.

'Bell!' He came charging over.

Shirley faded off somewhere.

'Wha'?'

'You writ that card yet?'

Jack faced him. Pride made him, but if this was going to come to a fight, it was going to happen when Betts wasn't around, too. Besides, Bennett was a bit right. Ivy Filer did need to know about the state of Shirley; someone was definitely scragging her.

'Gotta get a stamp. Me mum never stuck one on.'

'Then you get one, Bell. Ar'ter school. You get one, an' you get that card back to your 'ouse. Double quick.' Bennett stuck his face into Jack's, his hands gripped hard on Jack's collar. Jack smelt butcher's shop coming off them.

'Are you all right, Jack?' Clive had come to stand bravely close.

''E's all right. You mind yer own!' Bennett told him without looking round. 'Clear off!'

'I'll stand where I like.'

Jack didn't want a fight to happen. If a barney started here it would be Bennett and Betts against Bull and Ashwell – and Jack wasn't too smitten with Clive's chances. Woolwich boys had their own ways of fighting.

'Leave it, Clive. Ta. We're ... sorted out ...'

'Yeah, leave it, Clive,' Bennett repeated, 'fer yer own sake.'

Clive's eyes went wide bright, then narrowed to squints.

Before Clive could say something Jack quickly linked arms with him. 'Come on,' he said, and walked him away. ''E's all mouth an' trousers, that one. Not worth dustin' your knuckles.'

'I don't like bullies,' Clive said, trying to turn but not being allowed to.

'No, nor don't I, mate,' Jack agreed, walking them both on – not turning back at Bennett and Betts, either, but looking across the playground at Shirley Filer. 'Won't 'ave it. I won't 'ave it.'

The sound came into Jack's dream. A wasp? 'Wopsies' crawled all over the market fruit this time of year so you had to be careful where you sneaked your hand out for an apple. Jack woke up, waving his arms around his head to ward off any spiteful blighter. But it wasn't a wasp; the sound came from under his bed – and straight off he knew what it was; the secret buzzer; Clive was signalling. Jack rolled out of his sheets, waited for the buzzing to stop, and grabbed his own dynamo to run the wheel backwards and forwards across his carpet. He found his clothes in the dark – wasn't going to show a light round the crack of his bedroom door – pulled on his plimsolls, stuffed his pillow lengthwise under his bedclothes as if he was still asleep, and crept out of his room, keeping to the edge of the carpet.

Clive was at his door, dressed too, holding his torch.

'What is it?'

'That man you saw. Probably Parker...'

Definitely Parker, Jack thought. What with him having a secret code book and being a dodgy Londoner...

'I saw him from the bathroom window. He came through the grounds, went to the west ...'

Excitement pimpled Jack's skin. But he didn't know west from east. 'Which way's that?' he had to ask. 'Ain't got my bearings ...'

'Heading towards the woods. Come on, we'll follow him.'

'Yeah!' Jack had to turn a shiver into a little dance, but this was it! 'Which way out?'

'Back door. Like before.' Except that they hadn't

actually gone outside before. 'Come on.' Using his dimmed torch, Clive led the way downstairs and along through the kitchen to the back porch. Quietly, Clive turned the big key and slid the bolts aside.

A half moon shone from behind small clouds, but there was enough light for them to see where they were going – through spooky shadows among the shrubs, and across a clear paddock towards the boundary of Ashwell Hall and the edge of Mardenhurst Woods.

'Where d'you reckon he's going?' Jack whispered.

'He could take two directions in the woods. Come out on the Maidstone Road, or head off down towards Detling, past Red House Farm.'

Red House Farm! More ice for Jack. 'Hunden's!' he said. And there was no need to say any more to keep his eyes wide open – looking for a moon shadow that could be a German spy going to meet that farmer with the foreign seaman's voice.

Jack's nearest woods in Woolwich were Bostall Woods, where the locals said Dick Turpin used to hide out between his stage-coach robberies. But nowadays it had wide paths through it, more for short cuts than wild animals and hunters. Jack might play in them but he'd never been in the woods at night. These country woods, though, were the real thing, thick and overhanging, and in the dark you couldn't see where people trod. An owl hooted, very close – a scary sound like in a spooky film. And short squawks and shivery rustlings made him wish he'd put socks on under his plimsolls. He followed Clive closer than he'd want him to know, and his pride made him take a sharp step backwards whenever Clive stopped.

'Which way we goin'?'

'Sssh!'

'Sorry.'

'According to the moon we're heading west,' Clive whispered.

'The way he was goin' before?'

'If he hasn't doubled back ...'

Jack's head went down into his shoulders. *What if Parker had crept round after them, and was lurking right behind him?*

'We'll keep following the moon. We should come out at Parsonage Orchards – then we can see which way he's going through the apple trees.'

They went on, with still no sign of their man, Jack tripping a couple of times on tangled undergrowth, but mostly walking on wet leaves. His plimsolls were soaked through, his arms were scratched from the bramble bushes, his bare legs itched from nettles he hadn't spotted – and he realised how you didn't see everything at Saturday morning pictures, where cowboys did all this sort of thing and still looked dandy.

For a few minutes they had to stop because the moon had disappeared, and Clive wouldn't take a chance on being on track for heading west; he told Jack how going round large trees and clumps of undergrowth could take them on the wrong direction without realising; so they stood and listened, and the owl hooted first from Jack's left, then from behind him.

'You sure that's an owl? Not German signals?'

'That's a tawny, I know his sound.'

'Yeah, but – '

And, thank heavens, the moon came from behind a scud of cloud, and Clive led them on; but it had been a wise stop, because the moon wasn't shining from where Jack thought it should; they would have gone wrong. Now they came to the edge of the woods, and suddenly Jack understood what Clive had meant about seeing the man easier. In front of them lines of trees were planted in rows with spaces between them – and what was that in the far distance, moving away from them? A man. *The* man – because no one would be out apple-picking at this time of the night, would they?

He had to be the same man Jack had seen before; he was wearing that same raincoat and pulled-down hat, definitely looking more like a spy than a burglar, who'd be in a roll-necked sweater and a cap, with a bag in his hand.

'It's the farm that way,' Clive said. 'That's where he's heading. North-west. Along the Detling road.'

'Yeah.'

'Tree by tree,' Clive instructed Jack. 'Run to the first tree, stop behind it, check, run to the next, all the way down the line. That'll bring us out where he's going.'

'Right.'

'You take one side, I'll take the other.'

'Gotcha.'

One on each side of an avenue of apple trees, Jack and Clive darted, stopped, darted, stopped, and made good time running through the orchard in the direction the man had taken. There was no sign of him now – unless he had stopped and was waiting for them behind his own chosen tree. *With a hammer, or a bayonet, or a gun ...*

But there was no attack as the flitting moonlight guided them to the orchard gate on the far side; where, to Jack's surprise, they came out on the road by the bull's field; the road they'd walked from the top of The Street.

'He could've got here quicker on the road, but he didn't.' Clive turned to face Jack. 'Which proves he's a wrong-'un. He's decided to come the long, difficult way because he doesn't want to be spotted ...'

'Whoever he is ...'

'It's Parker. It's definitely Parker. There's no one else it can be, coming from where he's come from, where we both saw him, around the house. He'd have had to swim across the river, otherwise ...'

'Would he?' Jack still hadn't quite got his bearings.

They skulked along the hedgerow, doubled-over as they skirted Charlie the bull's field, coming to the tractor turn-in for Red House Farm.

And what was that, coming from a window high up in a barn opposite the farmhouse?

A flash. A quick flash of a torch, like someone answering a signal. And another. Then darkness.

'Hunden's up in the hay loft with his secret transmitter ...'

'... Ready to send secret stuff ...' Jack didn't want to bring Clive's Da's leather case into it. But he knew in his head what was going on, he'd gone to sleep the last couple of nights thinking about it. Parker was a pretend Londoner who said 'Tilbury Docks' instead of 'Chatham Docks' for rhyming slang, and he drove the colonel's car, carried his leather case, probably heard all sorts of secret army stuff being said. And Hunden was a new farmer in the village, with a Jerry-sounding name and a foreign voice. It all fitted for Jack. He and Clive stood and stared at each other again, eyes as big as full moons.

And that was when they heard the scream, coming from Hunden's farm.

Chapter Thirteen

'What was that?'

But Jack knew. It was Shirley. He'd known the sound of Shirley screeching from years back – she'd been a mizz-pot all her life because she was one of those kids things happened to. And something was happening to her right now.

'Shirley! Sounded like Filer.'

'Has he frightened her? Has Parker frightened her?'

'Dunno.' But Jack knew they couldn't run down to the farm to find out, they'd have to show themselves – and that would spoil their spy-tracking.

Instead, they crept as near to the farm buildings as they dared, edged down the cinder cart track keeping themselves nearer to the ground than the top of the hedgerow. The farmhouse was quite big, built in an 'L' shape, opposite which was the main barn and the milking sheds. The front door of the house was at the nearer end of the building; but what suddenly spilled out was light under the porch of the back door – and Shirley. She came running out, chased by someone who looked like Mrs Hunden – who was swiping at her with a knotted towel.

'Clumsy cow! Clumsy London cow! I've had that plate for years. *Years!* Best German porcelain.' She landed a swipe round the backs of Shirley's legs, bringing another loud scream. 'You'll pay for that! You'll pay for that plate!'

'Light! Mind that light!' This sounded like Hunden,

but Jack couldn't tell where the voice came from. All he knew was that Mrs Hunden went back indoors, the light went out, and Shirley, whimpering like in her baby days, went back inside as well.

'She was in her day clothes,' Clive said. 'Still working.'

'What time is it?'

'Well after midnight.'

'What we gonna do? Tell someone?'

Clive hunched himself down, thinking. 'We should. But if we tell anyone we'll have to give ourselves up for being here in the night – and we need more proof about the spying.'

Jack sat on the cinder track. 'Flashing a light's against the law.'

'But it's boys saying it, against a man. We need more than that to tell the Da …'

Jack sat thinking, too. 'Yeah, an' if we make a fuss about Shirley the Hun farmer's gonna know we're onto him …'

'We've got to leave things as they are till we're sure. Another day or so …'

'Keep our eyes open wi' matchsticks an' foller him again. The buzzer worked.'

'I knew it would.' Clive stood up. So … I'll watch from my window tonight, and see when Parker comes home. Log it.'

'Good idea.'

'Brief Wen in the morning.'

'Yeah.'

'We'll be off, then.' And Clive began a loping run back up the cinder track to the road, and, taking a chance in the quiet emptiness of Mardenhurst at night, he led them the quicker way home to Ashwell Hall and their separate bedrooms; where, within seconds, Jack's was reeking of sodden plimsolls.

Parker drove off the next morning to bring the colonel back to Ashwell Hall, which fitted in well with briefing Wendy. Clive did it as they ate their breakfast, sounding just like the colonel. He told her about the 'alert buzzer' working 'A-OK', the 'skilful Parker-stalking' and the 'safe- to-approach flashlight signal they'd seen'.

Wendy's eyes lit up. 'What an adventure! I should have been there. I must be there next time, you can't cut me out.'

But Clive hardly mentioned Shirley – and Jack had got out of bed feeling bad about her. No, he didn't like the girl; he'd had enough of her all his life, but she was from Woolwich, and these country people were knocking her about. He definitely ought to tell Mrs Rosewarn about it, because she'd soon put a stop to it. Or he ought to do something about it himself – like sending that postcard home, straight away.

'Clive, do you think there'll be medals for turning-in a nest of spies?'

'Probably, Wen. After the war. They'd keep it secret till then.'

A war medal for finding a spy! That sounded good to Jack. Fancy him wearing a gold medal around Woolwich! Also, when he thought about it, didn't people have to put up with nasty things happening to them to win a war? If Shirley got a medal, too, perhaps she wouldn't mind a bit of knocking-about for a couple more days.

She came to school that morning with Bennett and Betts. She was wearing thick stockings – to cover up her bruises, Jack reckoned – and her face looked nearly as old as her mother's. Jack pretended he hadn't seen her come into the playground – but Bennett had seen him, and he came bombing over.

'You get that stamp, Bell?'

'She was out of ha'pennies. Getting some today.'

Bennett didn't come back with words, he shoved his fist under Jack's nose. Jack stared him out, then walked away. He went into the boys' lavatories, chose a cubicle where the pan had been flushed, and stood there to think. He'd got to decide what he was going to do, and when. Should he tell old Stroker today about Shirley? The trouble was, if he did that he'd have to say he'd seen what happened at the farm instead of being in his bed. And whatever story he came up with, it would put the kibosh on following Parker – and then the spies could carry on with their spying. Or he could send the postcard home and get Ivy Filer down here – which would do the same thing – just a couple of days later, that was all. Or he could not do anything for a couple of days – and have a fight with Bennett.

Someone kicked the cubicle door so he pulled the chain. Or, there was one other thing that could happen. He and Clive could catch the spies quickly – in the time it took a postcard to get home and Ivy Filer to get down here. That would put a stop to what was happening to Shirley and to Bennett and Betts. And the more he thought about it, the more he thought that was what he'd bank on: Parker going out again in the next night or so.

He was in luck. Two things happened later that day. The car came back from Dover and as Jack and Clive got in from school the colonel was standing in the hallway, taking off his cap and wiping it round the inside.

'Good day at school, lads? You didn't put any tin spiders in the register, or buckets of water over the classroom door?'

They shook their heads – but Jack imagined what old Stroker would do if anyone tried to play any tricks on her.

Parker came wheezing in from the car carrying the colonel's leather case under his arm.

'Off the back seat, sir,' he said, handing it over.

'Thank you, Parker.' The colonel took it. 'I'll nip this upstairs.'

Jack took a quick look at Parker – who had to be staring at him at right that moment. It was one of those stares – mean, and nasty, and it was all Jack could do not to look away and stare at the leather case of army secrets under the colonel's arm.

'I'll put my plimsolls on,' he told Clive – and darted up the stairs. But as he went into his bedroom the colonel followed him up, and Lady Ashwell came along the landing.

'Here's to a good night's shut-eye, Sylv. No decent sleep to be had at Dover. Forty-eight hours' troop movements on the trot, and another forty-eight to come. It's dashed hard to keep the old eyeballs alight.'

Wow! That was really top secret, wasn't it? Jack closed his bedroom door as carefully as if it had a bomb

111

hanging on the hook. *Troop movements!* The colonel had been sending soldiers to secret places, and he was going to be doing some more the next day. And where our soldiers were being sent was just the sort of stuff the Jerries wanted to know. That's what they were listening out for. The posters on the stations said it. *'Keep it under your hat!' 'Careless talk costs lives!' 'Walls have ears!'* And some of those secret orders would definitely be in that leather case. Parker could easily have had a quick look in it. *And if he had, that would mean he'd be going down to Hunden's farm again tonight!*

But Jack sat tight on what he'd heard. He didn't want Clive to snitch his nose up and say his 'Da' would never leave secrets about. No, he decided, he'd wait and see what happened that night. If Parker had been digging his fingers into the colonel's leather case, the spies would want to jump quick. So when he went to bed he'd keep himself awake, and make sure that if Parker went out later, he'd be first to see him, and he'd buzz Clive instead of Clive buzzing him.

The sooner the spies got caught, the sooner he could start feeling better about Filer.

That night Jack wore his pyjamas over his clothes, so that lying in bed his top half looked normal. But he kept his sheet and blanket untucked, which meant he could keep slipping out of bed and dodging across to the window to look out. He was lucky that he didn't have the sort of blackout Clive and Wendy had – those black screens that fitted across their windows and had to be lifted up and down – because all he had to do to peep out was just pull his curtain back. But not for a bit; bedtime was nine o'clock so it was a waste looking out at first. The sun had gone down but the sky was still light, and the night before Parker had crept out when it was really dark. The trouble was, with a long time to wait there was a danger of him lying in bed and going off to sleep – so he checked and re-checked the buzzer and the dynamo, and placed and re-placed his plimsolls ready just inside the door, and said all his times tables, and tried to give himself a spelling test with awkward words like 'orkword'. But he did lose himself once, and suddenly sat up with a snort. He ran and checked at the window, but thank goodness it still wasn't quite dark yet. From then on, though, he sat cross-legged on the floor. If anyone came he'd pretend he was out of bed saying his prayers. He imagined that he was in the school hall at Union Street. He sang hymns inside his head – 'Onward Christian Soldiers' and 'For Those in Peril on the Sea' – and when he couldn't remember any more verses he checked again at the window. He told himself he was like a soldier on sentry duty up at the Royal Artillery, eyes open all night and his rifle ready. He was fighting for his country – fighting sleep so that he could help to catch a German spy – and whenever he looked up at his bed and thought how nice it would be to lie down and shut his eyes he kept himself awake by thinking of the medal he might get after the war, with his name on it. *Jack Bell, VC*. Wouldn't he get a clap in the hall for that!

Finally, when his backside had gone dead from sitting on the hard floor, he stood at the window peering out at the real dark, and he stared and stared and stared. And just when he couldn't stare any more, when his eyes had started to go blurry and he couldn't tell a tree from a tall man, he suddenly saw him! *Parker!* It had to be, in the same hat and coat he'd worn before, crossing the grass beneath the window and heading off in what Jack now knew was the direction of the woods. And Hunden's Farm!

Buzzer! Dynamo! Red alert for Clive!

Geronimo! Spiffo! Tonight's Parker-tracking was on!

Chapter Fourteen

Silent and still, Jack waited in Clive's room while he went for Wendy. He was back in no time, with Wendy dressed in a jumper and slacks and a Girl Guide belt around her waist on which was hooked a flat torch. They had both been as ready as him.

'It's the same bloke,' Jack hissed, 'wearing the same clobber, it's got to be.'

'He's got a five minute start on us,' Clive said, 'which'll have him deep into Mardenhurst Woods by now. But we know where he's going, so we can cut along the road and beat him to it – hide in the hedge by Charlie's field.' And he led them off, down the stairs like burglars, out through the scullery door and along the drive, running them at a good pace down the Detling road.

As it turned out, when they got to Charlie's field they didn't have too much time to spare. The man had made good time through the woods and the orchard, and they hadn't long settled down with no more wriggling and no more whispering, when they heard a clump as a foot hit the top of the orchard gate – and there he was in his raincoat and hat. And there, without any doubt now, was the face Jack expected to see, and the sound of wheezing that went with it. Parker. It was definitely Parker. The sudden sight of him made Jack want to wee – but he didn't, just about holding it off because if he'd wet himself it would have looked like he was scared. Which he was: there was something dead evil about Parker; he looked spiteful and nasty like the spies and crooks they had in films, and Jack could just imagine him coming into his bedroom in the middle of the night and reaching out his strong, German hands …

Wendy made a little noise, but it could have been a creature in the hedgerow, and Parker didn't seem to take any notice. He pulled down his hat and loped off along the lane towards the farm, taking a torch out of his raincoat pocket as he went; and after a count of a hundred from Clive – counted properly in seconds like a soldier, no speeding up at the end – the three of them followed, Jack last and catching up, after weeing on a patch of dandelions.

He was just in time to see the same flash of light from the house. Parker must have shone his torch first, and this was the reply. 'A-OK to approach,' as Clive would say. His eyes hurting with staring into the gloom, Jack watched to see what would happen next. Would Shirley get chased out again, and whacked for doing something wrong? But tonight the house seemed very quiet. In the shadows, though – and it was hard to see – he thought he could just make out a couple of figures flitting across the yard towards one of the barns. But he couldn't be sure – and he definitely couldn't see who they were.

'Transmitter's in the hay loft,' Clive said. He had seen what Jack had seen. 'Part of the network. Parker daren't risk having one at the Hall.'

'Extra clever,' Wendy added. 'If anyone gets suspicious, all they've got to do is start a fire. Barns go up like billy-o.'

'Cunning. Hide by destroying.'

'Spy stuff,' Jack explained, as if he'd been in the Secret Service all his life.

'Well,' Wendy said, 'we either go forward and creep into the barn to listen, or we get back home, think about our best next moves. We won't see much more crouching here.'

Jack waited to see what Clive would say. He knew what he fancied doing – or, rather what he *didn't* fancy – getting trapped by Parker in that barn.

Clive made the decision. 'We go home,' he said. 'Parker could be five hours in there or he could be five minutes, it depends what decoding and transmitting they've got to do.'

'I don' mind hanging on ...' Jack lied.

'We go home tonight, but we take it in turns to wait up and watch every night from now on. Then from the minute he goes out, we'll know we've got time to search his room...'

'Do what?' *Search Parker's room?* 'Who?'

'One of us.'

'Why?'

'Looking for what, exactly?' Wendy wanted to know. 'We've already found the notebook in the stables...'

'Newspaper stuff to transmit, that sort of thing,' Clive told her. 'He might not risk anything as big as a transmitter – but he could have an English-German dictionary, or a marked map of Kent ...'

'Or a secret uniform to wear under his clothes for when the Jerry parachutes come down,' Jack joined in.

'It won't be anything big. He's keeping himself clean by hiding his notebook in the stables. But it'll be something that sticks out ...'

'Oooer! But how do we get into his room? He's bound to lock it when he goes out.'

'Easy!' Clive told Wendy. 'Ma's got spare keys to everywhere, they're in the kitchen wall cupboard. Every door in the place, in case of fire, theft, or emergency.'

Jack knew this to be true, he had seen them all hanging up. But there being a key to get into Parker's room wasn't really what was bugging him. It was who was going to have to do the search. And that was the thought running through his head all the way back to Ashwell Hall and to bed. They had made it out and back twice in two nights. But how long would they get away with Lady Ashwell, and Florrie, and the colonel if he was home, not waking up and checking on one of them in the night? Or hearing them creeping down or up the stairs? Or especially one of them creeping across the courtyard to Parker's room on top of the stables; whoever had to do that …

Jack lied to Bennett the next day. Well, spies had to tell lies, and he was a spy for our side, wasn't he? He was ready for the beefy boy when he came over to him in the playground next morning; and instead of giving him back a fist under his throat, when he was asked the question he knew was coming, he just put up both his thumbs.

'You get that stamp?'

Up went the thumbs.

'You writ that card?'

Jack put up one thumb again, then the other.

'What's that mean?'

'What d'you think?'

'You done it, 'ave you?'

Jack showed him his two thumbs again. He had done stuff, hadn't he? His thumbs didn't have to be saying exactly what.

'You better 'ave.'

Jack waggled the thumbs like two little puppets saying 'watch what I'm saying'.

'Or else!' Bennett said. 'Or I'll stick them thumbs where you'll never get 'em out!'

At school dinnertime Jack made sure to sit next to Shirley. He didn't explain himself to Clive, he just did it. One reason was Bennett. When Bennett saw him sitting next to Shirley he'd think he was telling her he'd sent a postcard home, to tell Ivy Filer what was going on at Hunden's Farm. The other reason was to find out what Shirley really wanted him to do; to feel better inside for letting her go on getting hit while he went on with his secret spy stuff. Of course, he couldn't let on about that – although he'd like to know if she'd seen a man coming to the farm in the night, and going over into the barn.

But he'd only just got the word 'postcard' out when she turned her long, miserable face to him. 'Don' you do nothing,' she said. 'Forget Bennett – he wants that card sent for him, not for me.' She looked really scared. 'You 'aven't sent it, 'ave you?' Jack shook his head, keeping it low. 'If they thought my mum was coming down to get me they'd know from the council lady first 'cos she'd need help finding the farm, an' they'd say they'd never done nothing. They'd tell her I was getting my own back for them getting cross when I broke something.' She dropped her voice. 'An' that Eva can hit you so it don't show ...'

Jack blew out his cheeks. So he'd been right not to send a postcard for Shirley. But he was still going to cop it from Bennett if he didn't. Help! Life was a real mix-up. Being down in the country was supposed to be safe, but he was in a big a fix right now as ever he'd been in Woolwich.

What about Parker, though – what did she know about a man coming in the night? But he wasn't going to find out right then. They were all sitting at the trestle tables waiting to be called up for their dinners from Mrs Newbold the cook when Miss Buckshoot blew her whistle and came forward to stand in the middle of the hall for Grace.

'Let us pray,' she said. 'What you are about to receive from God and courtesy of Mrs Newbold is meat and vegetables, and you will have a sufficiency. No one will rise from the table with a vole of hunger gnawing in their stomach. But this is wartime. Soon – if things happen again as they did in the Great War – food will be rationed. German submarines will patrol our coast and meat and wheat from the Empire will be in short supply. You will be allowed only meagre amounts of meat and sugar and bread, just enough to keep you alive. Our farms and our butchers and grocers will be under strict control. So we must thank God for what we are about to receive today ...'

'Which is getting cold,' Mrs Newbold said.

'Dear God,' Miss Buckshoot went on, glowering at her.

And Jack didn't get to find out anything more

about Parker at the farm in the night because it was all 'go' – being called up to the counter and queuing – when Shirley got away from him and sat somewhere else with her plate of precious food.

Wendy was busy while Jack and Clive were at school. When they came home she told them how Parker had come back from Dover and had reminded her mother that it was actually his half-day off. He wheeled his bike out of the stables, and went off down the drive. So she had pretended to need a new bottle of ink and got out her bike, too, and followed him.

'Guess where he went?' she asked when they couldn't be overheard, picking up windfalls in the orchard.

'Not the farm?' Clive said.

'No.'

'To some other village where there's another spy?' Jack guessed. 'I bet there's hundreds of 'em all over the place …'

Wendy shook her head. 'No. He went to Riversmeet Station, where you came to, Jack. He padlocked his bike to the railings and got on a train. To – '

'London!'

'Spot on, Jack. And he's not back yet.'

Jack bit into a sweet russet. 'He's got spy bosses up London, I'll tell you. An' they let him know what stuff he's got to find out …'

'Find out from where?' Clive asked. 'More likely, they're telling him the secrets he's got to send out. That's what he's got written in code in his notebook. Probably secrets to send out to a submarine in the

Channel. It comes up at a certain time, and Parker and Hunden transmit to it, short range, when there's less chance of interception from all the radio stations. He gets given information from spies in the Admiralty, or the Air Force ...'

'Or the army.' But Jack didn't like to say what secrets he really thought Parker was sending. He liked old Clive, but he knew all right. Parker drove their 'Da' around, and the colonel was a top bloke at Dover Castle, sending soldiers' regiments to different places. And he'd had his eyeballs in that leather case the day before. Plus, at Dover Parker definitely had to see stuff and hear stuff – like when you're made to stand outside the staffroom door at school.

'Anyhow, we'll all keep *cavey* tonight. If he's got new secrets to send, that's our chance to search his room ...'

Jack's stomach turned over. Just as long as it didn't have to be him doing the searching. That was going a scary bit too far ...

But it didn't happen, not that night. Parker came back and had some supper in the kitchen at the same time as Jack and the others were having theirs. And he was a very good spy, Jack started thinking, he sounded very normal, talking about getting new brake blocks for his bike – until he told Florrie that he'd been to see his "skin an' blister" in Peckham. 'I like to keep in touch with her, she's all on her "Tod Sloan".' *He's overdoing the cockney stuff!* Jack thought. And real cockneys didn't say *all* the rhyme; they'd just say she's 'on her Tod', not the full 'Tod Sloan'. And when he said it, he stared at Jack again with those nasty eyes and put a twist on his mouth, as if he was reminding him he knew how to kick hard where it hurt.

And after watching and waiting cross-legged on his bedroom floor until he'd given up and climbed into bed, Jack was relieved to wake up in the dead of night and realise that the buzzer hadn't sounded, and he hadn't had to buzz Clive. So Parker hadn't gone out – and no one was going to have to be the one to search the Jerry spy's room.

Chapter Fifteen

Bennett was waiting for Jack. As he and Clive went into the playground next morning, the bully-boy came steaming over. Both his ears were blood red as if he'd had them half twisted off, and the skin around his eyes was swollen like mouldy apples.

He pushed Clive out of the way and swung Jack around to face him. 'You never sent it, did you? All your "thumbs up" crap – you lyin' little turd!'

'Who said I never sent it?'

'Shirley.' Bennett suddenly punched Jack in the stomach, no warning, just *whack!* – pitching him back against the school fence.

Doubled over, winded and desperately sucking in breath, Jack pulled himself up. *Right!* He never started fights: he was small and he lived off his wits, so he never went round looking for a barney – knowing when to run, where to hide, what lies to tell, how to keep his head down, that was how he got by. But if someone else started a fight he stood his ground until he was flattened.

Taking air in through his nose so he could keep his jaw tight, he pushed himself off the fence and lunged back at Bennett. One of those ears was sitting up and begging for a good right hook.

But not for long. Suddenly Clive was swinging Bennett around to face him instead. 'Musketeers!' he shouted into his face. 'All for one and one for all!' His fists clenched, he levelled his left arm at Bennett's head and tucked his right fist back against his cheek.

Holding his body straight, he danced forward and back in front of the meaty boy, in his range and out of it, looking like a boxer in a ring – about to be flattened.

'Watch out!' Jack shouted. Clive was as tall as Bennett but he was going to get mashed. Bennett was from Union Street, and if Clive thought he could fight clean against a street scrapper he was wrong. Bennett would spit, claw, butt, and kick; and if he got Clive down on the ground he'd stamp on his head.

Bennett swore and went at Clive with a sneering look at the fancy way the country boy was facing up. But Clive was giving himself room, keeping his left arm outstretched on a level with Bennett's chin; and as the big boy came within range he jabbed three times at his snorting nose – two of the three hitting the target – and straight-off Bennett's face was pouring with blood. Bennett cuffed it, saw the damage on his sleeve. He swore again, and came in sideways, catching Clive off balance with a wild swing. Clive recovered and started dancing at him again, but Bennett put his thick neck down and charged in like a bull, wildly aiming a hefty punch that landed on Clive's shoulder and rocked him back.

'What did I tell you?' Jack yelled. 'What did I show you?'

Clive didn't seem to have heard; his chin was tucked in as he held his head down and concentrated on Bennett, staring into his eyes.

'Drippy little country kid!' Bennett growled, and with both arms outstretched he went for Clive's throat – but his grasping hands couldn't get there before Clive suddenly dropped his boxer's stance, put in a shuffle step, and aimed a flying kick, just the way Jack had shown him, catching Bennett on the chest.

'Aaagh!'

This gave Clive the split-second he needed to send a straight right at Bennett's head, catching him hard on the cheek and twisting his face into rubber.

'Yow!'

People were running across the playground – to see Bennett staggering back and swearing insults at Clive.

'Stop! Stop at once!'

A loud whistle blew: and there was Mrs Rosewarn, alight with anger, grabbing hold of Bennett's neck with one hand and Clive's with the other.

'Disgusting! How dare you! What sort of hospitality is this?' she shouted into Clive's face.

Bennett stopped, stooped and held there, his chest heaving, his face still twisted, his nose gushing with blood. But Clive held his head high and put up his guard again. Mrs Rosewarn shook his neck from side to side. 'Into the hall, boy! Stand at the front and wait for me!' She released Bennett's neck. 'Take yourself to the lobby and lie down on the cold floor, head back.' She turned to one of the older girls. 'Vickery – go to the staffroom and ask Mrs Fossdyke to kindly administer first aid to Bennett.'

'Yes, Miss.' Maureen Vickery ran off into the school building.

'And the rest of you, disperse!'

When Jack went into the school hall, Clive was at the front, standing to attention like a soldier. The rest came in with 'you're-in-for-it-now' jibes from the Woolwich boys, which Jack tried to shut up; but other than that he didn't know what to do. He was in this with Clive, so should he go and stand next to him, or should he sit at his desk?

He went to the front: they were the Two Musketeers, weren't they? If Clive was in trouble, he'd got to be, too. He'd started Bennett off by not sending the postcard so it was his fight really, not Clive's.

Clive didn't look at him, didn't change the way he was staring straight ahead, but, 'Sit down!' he hissed from the side of his mouth.

Jack teetered. He'd like to sit down, old Stroker could really dish them out when she was snorting angry. But if he could tell her how Bennett had started the fight he might take a bit of the swish out of what she was going to do. He stayed – and feeling like the best mate a kid could ever have, he stood and stared at the back wall the same way as Clive was doing.

Some coughing and a lot of sitting up told him that Mrs Rosewarn had come in behind him.

'Bell – sit down!' And a clout round the back of his head told him just how swished up she was.

'Please, Miss …'

Another clout. 'Sit down!'

Jack went back to his place. From his seat he could see Stroker and who was with her – Bennett, holding a piece of rag to his nose, and being shown to his desk as if he was the Mayor of Woolwich.

'Keep your head back, and try not to swallow.'

'Yes'm.'

'And I'll find some Vaseline for those mauled ears.'

Jack wanted to stand up and tell her those mauled ears were sweet fanny to do with Clive, Bennett had brought them to school with him. He looked around at Betts and at Shirley Filer, but neither of them moved or said anything, they just sat there watching like everybody else.

'Now!' Mrs Rosewarn marched to the front of the hall. 'You, boy!'

'Miss?' said Clive, with a little click of his heels.

The teacher took in a deep breath and went up onto her toes. 'My London children, refugees from a second Great War, displaced from their homes by the threat of enemy action, missing their mothers who are far away – these poor souls have come here for safety and friendship. And what do you have to offer them? Pugilism! Enmity! This morning you have drawn more blood on these shores than Adolf Hitler has managed so far, and you shall pay for it!' Her face was red, and her words were coming out on little bullets of spit. 'Wait there!'

Jack knew only too well what would happen next. *The poor old Musketeer,* he thought – Stroker hadn't calmed down an inch, she'd worked herself up a yard-and-a-half. And his mouth went dry as she stomped across to the door and from behind the roller towel hanging on it, she whisked out her cane. Back she came, swishing it through the air to make it flex and whistle.

'Six!' she said. 'And think yourself lucky it's not twelve!'

Clive pulled himself up straighter still. His face was white and his eyes looked scared. Jack could tell that he'd never had the cane before: the ruler perhaps, or a floppy plimsoll on his bum, but not the real thing.

'Hand up, arm out, palm straight and level!'

Clive took up the punishment position. He might never have had it, but he knew how it was done.

'Hold yourself still.' Mrs Rosewarn took a step back to line herself up for the first stroke. 'I shall teach you how to welcome London's evacuees!'

'*You will not!*' A loud voice came booming from the back of the hall. Everyone twisted – but they all knew who this was. Miss Buckshoot had come in from her classroom, dislodging children at their desks as she came through and marched to the front. 'What is this about?'

For a second it looked as if Mrs Rosewarn might give Miss Buckshoot a whack instead of Clive.

'This boy has bloodied the nose and mauled the ears of one of my pupils …' Stroker's voice was high with anger; Jack knew it well.

'*Clive? Clive Ashwell?* Have you asked him for any sort of an explanation?' The Mardenhurst teacher's voice was low and snorty. 'Has he been offered common justice? There are two sides to every wrangle.'

'And there are two eyes in my head with perfect vision, and I saw what I saw through each of them.'

Miss Buckshoot wore glasses; thick, horny ones. She took in a deep breath and filled out her large blouse. 'I have no problem with my corrected eyesight, and none with my sense of fairness. And I am the headmistress here. If there is to be a caning in this school the punishment book is to be sent for.'

Jack could hardly believe what he was hearing. Teachers didn't argue with one another, they backed each other up. If a kid was in trouble between teachers he got a double dose, just to make sure. But these two were standing there like two market women in Beresford Square arguing over an inch of stall space.

Miss Buckshoot turned to Clive, who had put down his arm. 'Clive Ashwell, explain yourself, please.'

'I can – ' Mrs Rosewarn began, but Miss Buckshoot held up a hand and gave a short, sharp, '*Shush!*'

Clive waited until Miss Buckshoot nodded for him to speak. 'Bennett punched Jack Bell in the stomach, he started it. Bell was too hurt to hit back – ' Jack shook his head – 'so I took Bennett on for him.' He paused for a second, as if he knew that what he was about to say would be a clincher. 'Jack Bell is our guest at Ashwell Hall. We're best friends.'

Jack's mouth went dry, and his eyes pricked.

'There!' Miss Buckshoot's voice was triumphant. 'A Mardenhurst boy coming to the aid of a London boy.' She stared at Mrs Rosewarn. 'Isn't that what we should all be wishing for in these difficult days?' Mrs Rosewarn went to speak, but Miss Buckshoot held up her hand. 'He was being bullied by one of his own.'

Mrs Rosewarn turned fast to face the class. With her cane pointing she singled out big, soft, Eric Platt. 'Platt – did you see any of this?'

'A bit, Miss.' Eric Platt stood to attention; his eyes on Bennett, not on the teacher.

'And …?'

Right then Bennett didn't look much of a threat to anyone; he was still holding his head back and dabbing at his nose with the reddening rag, a sight that seemed to Jack to give Eric Platt a bit of ginger.

'What I saw, Miss, Bennett did touch Bell.'

'*Did touch?*'

'Yes, Miss.'

'And with what did he touch?'

'His fist, Miss.'

'You mean, he punched him?'

'Sort of, Miss.'

'Then say so. Sit down.'

Without a word Mrs Rosewarn laid her cane across her desk.

But, 'I am not proud of you,' Miss Buckshoot told Clive. 'You should not be descending to gutter-fighting levels. You should have come for me, which would have been the civilized Mardenhurst way of doing things, wouldn't it? I shall have to write to your mother, of course.' She turned to Mrs Rosewarn. 'Clive's mother is our Chairman of Managers. She will need to know of this incident between our sets of pupils.'

To this, Mrs Rosewarn's rolled her head like a loose puppet, a '*don't-think-that-cuts ice with me*' sight Jack knew all too well from when he was feeding her a cock-and-bull story.

Clive was sent to his place and Miss Buckshoot went back to her classroom. Mrs Rosewarn had opened the register and ripped the top off her pen as if it was someone's head. And for the rest of the morning it wasn't easy for Jack or anyone else to get down to any English or Arithmetic.

Never mind the Germans, the war was hotting up.

Chapter Sixteen

Lady Ashwell was not pleased with either of them; not pleased with Clive when she read the letter he had brought home from school, and not pleased with Jack, going by the look she gave him. 'I wrote to tell your mother how well you'd fitted in,' she said, immediately turning to Clive. 'We need to talk about this,' she said sternly. 'Alone.'

That made Jack feel bad. Wasn't he supposed to be family? Wasn't she supposed to be Aunt Sylvia – even though he could never force himself to call her that? But now, the first time there was a little spot of bother, she'd started treating him like a stranger, cutting him out of things. Or like Parker – who wasn't allowed to sit down in the house unless he was told he could. The toffs and the toe-rags!

He watched as she led off towards the drawing room, Clive following on like a servant himself. He heard the door shut. The drawing room was just past the stairs at the front of the house so on his way to change into his plimsolls Jack only had to go a couple of steps to press his ear to the door. But it was solid wood and he couldn't hear as much as he'd have liked. But what he did hear made his nose turn up. He heard his name – and he heard it a lot. 'Jack *this*' … 'Jack *that*' … 'Jack *something else* …' First it was Clive saying it, then it was her – saying it, and saying it, and saying it 'Jack', 'Jack', 'Jack' – and once, 'the Londoner.' 'And when all the drone was finished her voice went louder and he heard her say, 'You've changed, Clive, and not for the better!' Her voice suddenly went quiet and Jack dodged away, was halfway up the stairs when the drawing room door opened. 'Just remember what I've said to you!'

Jack dived into his room and shut the door. *Right!* he thought. It didn't take long for the skin to get scraped off the rice pudding, did it? One titchy thing happened at school and Jack Bell was in the dog house – just because he didn't come from round here. And the trouble was, it would always be the same. It didn't matter where he went or what he did – to these posh people a kid like him was like a cat with a tin tied to its tail: *watch out! Here comes a London flea-bag!*

Well – he knew what he would do about that! He was Jack Bell, and he definitely didn't have to hang around down here where he wasn't wanted. But before he could sit on his bed and plan exactly what he was going to do there was a tap on his door.

It was Clive. He came into the bedroom trying to look all relaxed, as if he wasn't bothered about anything in the world, as if he'd just been having a cup of tea with his Ma.

'Get a good rollicking, did you?'

'Not really. Ma's just a bit upset because old Buckshoot thought I'd let myself down. She says with her being Chairman of the Managers I've got to show exemplary behaviour at school.'

Jack didn't know what 'examplary' meant, but he could guess. It didn't mean fight anyone who had a go at their evacuee. 'No rough old mates, then ...'

Clive took a bit too long to answer. 'I definitely

133

mustn't get into fights in the playground, especially with – '

'Us lot?' Jack pulled on his plimsolls and kept his head down – until Clive didn't answer. He stood up. 'Anyhow, I could've sorted Bennett myself, I was just getting my breath back. He give me a right crafty one in the guts …'

Clive backed off and went to stand by the door. 'Anyway, we're still the Two Musketeers, Jack. "One for all and all for one."'

'Yeah, with knobs on.'

'I'll see you at tea-time, then.'

'Definite.'

Clive went, and Jack sat on his bed again. So, no windfall collecting or games in the garden this afternoon. Clive was probably going to go and play with his soldiers' band. All of which left Jack feeling really on his own – for the first time since he'd come here.

OK, fair enough, he knew where he wasn't wanted, and he'd already made up his mind. He hadn't been going to stay down here for long, anyway. Right from the start he'd had it in his head to get back to Woolwich where the schools were all closed. And when he walked in on his mother and he told her about Shirley – and Ivy Filer came down here to take her home – she'd definitely let him stay. She'd have to, wouldn't she?

He checked his suitcase, and feeling secretive like Parker, he sorted the things he needed to take with him – like his clothes and his torch and his gas mask – and made sure that they were packed. But he wasn't going to be stupid. He wasn't going to go off in the night and hang around in the woods until the morning, then start finding his way home. And he couldn't take his suitcase with him when he went to school, they'd all know he was going on the run if he did that. No, he'd have to give it until Saturday morning, when all of a sudden, blow me down, that toe-rag Jack Bell wouldn't be here any more.

He'd be heading back to where he belonged.

When the noise first sounded Jack was in a weird sleeping fantasy where he was on his way to London sitting in the back of the Austin Cambridge – which was being driven by Mrs Rosewarn, of all people. At first the thing he was hearing was the car horn being blown at Charlie the bull, standing smack in the middle of The Street, but as the noise went on he woke up properly. *'The buzzer!'* Clive was sending him an alert. Now he had to get his pyjamas off and some clothes on, because he hadn't gone to bed ready for a call-out. All the same, he was dressed and in Clive's bedroom within a couple of minutes. Wendy was in her dressing gown and nightie, but Clive was dressed for action.

'Parker!' Clive said. 'He's just gone off again. Didn't you see him on your side?'

'Couldn't. I was under my bed checking the buzzer wires.'

'Ah.'

'All working A-OK.'

'Right. That gives us an hour at least, I think. We've never seen what time he comes back, but it must take a while to encode messages and transmit them …'

'Or receive them, more probably,' Wendy put in. 'He hasn't been to London today.'

And he hasn't driven the car to get the colonel, Jack thought – but he kept that to himself.

'So one of us must search his room.' Clive looked at Wendy – in her nightclothes – and at Jack. 'Wendy will get the key, then Jack or I will do our patriotic duty …'

Jack had gone cold. His stomach would have turned over if it hadn't been frozen. Creeping across the courtyard to the stables, going up the iron staircase, creeping into Parker's room, that was dangerous stuff. That was real. And whoever did it would be on his own doing it.

'Shall we draw lots?' Clive asked.

'What's that?'

'Dip. Ick-ack-ock, best of three. Spin a coin.'

'Oh, right.'

Clive was staring back at him with his head up and his chin out, the way he'd stood waiting for the cane in the school hall – brave, the way he'd been ready to take his strokes for jumping in and helping him.

Jack looked back at him, lifted his own head. 'I'll go.' He couldn't believe he'd just heard himself saying that. But he had, it was out, he'd said it. Even if he hadn't had the stick, Clive had taken the can for him with his Ma – and now he would take it for Clive.

But he'd just put himself up for the most dangerous thing they'd done since they'd been certain Parker was a German spy.

'Good man!'

'I'll get the key.' Wendy slipped out of the bedroom.

Jack wished she'd said something more than that – he was being a blooming hero, wasn't he? Didn't she know he never put up his hand for anything, not when he was all right in the head. But this wasn't only for Clive, this was over Lady Ashwell. He was in the dog house with her, he was the kid who was a bad influence on her son; and he didn't like that. But what sort of an influence would he be on *everything* if he came out of Parker's room with something to prove he was spying for the Germans? He'd get that medal, and Lady Ashwell would be as proud as Punch to know Jack Bell the Woolwich boy.

'Have you got your torch?'

''Course.'

'Then we'll creep down to the kitchen and rendezvous with Wendy and the key ...'

'OK.'

'And you know what to do? What we're looking for?'

'Dodgy stuff ...'

'But don't touch it. Just note it. Da and the police will find it when you tell them where it is. And be careful over lights and blackout. All clear?'

'Yup.' Jack sounded a lot more up for this than he felt.

'Keep *cavey*.'

Jack checked outside the bedroom door. The landing was quiet, and Florrie's room was on the next floor up. Quietly, like before, Jack and Clive crept down the stairs to the kitchen – where Wendy was waiting for them, holding up a long key as if it was a dodgy discovery in itself.

'Don't lose it.' She gave it to Jack, who put it in his trouser pocket.

'Well done, Jack.' Clive sounded just like his father.

'Out through the scullery, and back the same way. We'll be keeping watch from the drawing room.'

'OK.' For a second Jack stood there as if his feet were set in concrete. He didn't want to go, he didn't want to do this – but in a mad fit he had said that he would. Now it was too late to back out. He took in a brave-sounding breath. He'd got to prove to these people that Woolwich kids were as good as any soldier, and anyone's 'Da'. And when Jack said he'd do something, he did it. You didn't have to be what Florrie called 'gentry' to keep a promise.

Although he wished like heck that he hadn't opened his big mouth …

Chapter Seventeen

The courtyard had paving stones not shingle so Jack's plimsolls made no noise as he went slowly on his toes across to the stables. It was a cloudy night and he had to stare his eyes hard to see where he was going. Every door in this place had an electric lantern over the top of it but in the blackout they were all kept switched off. So although he wanted to run fast across the courtyard, he daren't. 'Black as pitch,' he could hear his mother say. And wouldn't it be great if it really was his own door he was heading for instead of a dirty spy's.

The iron stairs up to the room were steeper than he'd thought. Once at the top he had to use his torch. Where was the keyhole? He couldn't find it with his fingers – and no wonder, because when he gave the door the quickest of flashes he saw that it was hidden behind a little piece of leather to stop light from shining through it. *A spy working in the night would think of that.* He held the key right ready to push into the lock – and he stopped. Up to now he hadn't done anything wrong, had he? Being out of bed in the night wasn't *wrong* wrong – not *police* wrong. Neither was being up at the top of these stairs; he could say Wendy's ball had bounced up here and he'd promised to get it back – he was just afraid to come up in the daytime when Mr Parker was about. Up to this minute he could only get into trouble for behaving like a Simple Simon. But once he put this key into the lock and he turned it, and definitely once he went into Parker's room, if he got caught he'd be right in the doghouse.

He stood still and counted to ten, the way Clive would. And on 'nine' he decided that none of all that mattered if he came back out of here able to tell everyone that Parker had got German stuff inside. Being a hero in the war gave you the right to do wrong things.

OK! Now! He pushed the key into the lock, turned it, and it opened smoothly as if the lock was well-oiled. And now he had to be well-oiled himself. He was going to go in. But a scary thought suddenly hit him. *He* hadn't seen Parker go out, and he'd only got Clive's word that he'd seen Parker under his window. What if it hadn't been Parker but someone else? What if it had been one of those real burglars this time, and not a spy? What if Parker was still in here, ready to jump out of bed and grab him? The thought was enough to make him turn that key back the other way and get off back to the house.

But he didn't. He held his breath, pushed on the door, and took a step inside.

It was dead quiet, and very dark. A first action would be to put his hand up to find a light switch, but he'd got hold of himself well enough to know that he mustn't do that. He'd got a torch. All the same, he felt for the switch anyway, just in case. There were two switches next to one another; had to be one for inside and one for the light at the top of the stairs. Quietly, gently, he pushed the door almost closed behind him; leaving it open just a crack so that he could get out without fumbling around for the handle. It was so quiet that he heard an owl from over in the woods – 'whoo-oo' – a sound that nearly sent him out again, all by itself.

It wasn't a big room – and what was there? A bed took up most of the space, at the bottom of which was a small armchair tucked into an alcove – and along from it was a small chest-of-drawers with a washing jug and bowl on it. Coming along the other wall and leading back towards the door, was a cupboard with a gas ring and a kettle on top; then there was the window, with the same sort of blackout screen as Clive had; and, near the door again, was a small wardrobe. Altogether, the place wasn't much bigger than Jack's own room at home.

But – very different from his – Parker's room was neat and tidy. There were no clothes over the chairs, the blanket on the bed wasn't rucked up, and apart from the kettle and the wash jug everything was inside something else. There were no dishes or plates and no old newspapers or clobber on the table, and no hangers of clothes on the outside of the wardrobe. Where to look first, then? Well, under the bed would be a good place. There, and on top of the wardrobe were always good places for secrets. But he didn't fancy bending down to look; it didn't feel safe, him not being on his feet, and crouching with his back to the door. *Because what if Parker hadn't gone to the farm, and he'd heard him coming, and he was lying under the bed like a dead body – or one of those monsters that reach out and get you?*

But he'd got to do it – or he might as well not have come. There could be a suitcase under here with a Nazi armband in it for when the paratroops dropped down.

Without daring to think any more about it he bent down and shone a glimmer of light under the bed. And what he saw there was the one thing he'd reckon to see in most bedrooms, a po for Parker to use in the night.

Jack got quickly to his feet again and went for the wardrobe next, took a step towards it, shone his torch – and, *help!* He jumped, both feet off the floor, his skin freezing. Someone was standing there: not Parker, but someone fierce-looking – staring straight at him! He backed off, tripped on a rug – but a great gush of relief he realised that it wasn't a man. It was Jack Bell, reflected in the mirror on the front of Parker's wardrobe door. *'Crikey Dick!'* He stood there and tried to take down some deep breaths, made himself wait for his body to calm. He could feel the thumping of his heart, and the prickling of the goose-pimples on his arms. Who needed frights like that? He wanted to pack this in, and tell Clive he just hadn't found anything.

Except – he'd half done his job, hadn't he? He was in, it was only quick looks in the wardrobe, chest-of-drawers and cupboard, and he could get out of here. Slowly, he reached for the catch to the wardrobe door, turned it ready to pull it open. And – *no!* – it came swinging open and caught him on the shoulder. Another scare – but only a second's worth. He knew right off there wasn't anyone in there pushing out; at Union Street they had a wobbly cupboard whose door did the same thing. But it was another skin-freeze, another heart-thump.

Inside the wardrobe it was all as neat as the rest of the room. Parker's raincoat wasn't there, but hanging up was the dark suit he wore for driving. At the bottom was a pair of shoes, but no newspaper stuff, or dictionary, or map of Kent – and definitely no German army boots, radio transmitter, Nazi helmet, pistol, bayonet, or swastika armband.

Chests-of-drawers had good places for hiding secrets – stuff tucked into socks or under the old newspapers that lined them. He crept over to the it. Even by the skinny light from his torch he could see how it was shinier than the other bits of furniture – so it could be that it had more special stuff in it. Anyhow, it was his best chance, he reckoned.

He bent to the bottom drawer and opened it – where there were a couple of pairs of pants and socks. He squeezed them for anything hidden but there was nothing. Leaving it as tidy as he could he opened the next one up – which had vests, a pullover, and a thick jumper that wanted to spring out. Again he squeezed and prodded, but there was nothing a spy would have in here, and, forcing the jumper down, he pulled out the middle drawer.

'Well, well, well – what have we got in here?'

Jack froze and just about melted, both at once. He couldn't move, not to stand, not to roll over, not to open his mouth. *That hadn't been him speaking!* It had been Parker, who was standing there in the doorway.

'You thievin' London toe-rag!' Parker shut the door behind him, came across the room and switched on his bedside lamp. 'You little sewer rat!'

Jack could only squeak, and just about swallow. What could he say? *Why the devil could he have been up here?*

Parker stared down at him, looking all the more

deadly for standing there for a good ten seconds, silent in his raincoat and hat.

'What's your game, then? Up to your tea-leaving tricks?' He took off his trilby hat and wiped the inside of the rim with a handkerchief, going slowly round and round.

Jack had got to say something. You had to have a go at an excuse or people knew you were guilty straight off. 'Wendy's ball. Thought Wendy's ball come in your window 's'afternoon an' you was keepin' it ...'

Parker changed the angle of his neck to one that said this was a load of lying codswallop. Silently undoing the buttons and loosening the belt, he took off his raincoat and folded it very neatly and slowly, all the while staring hard at Jack. Underneath he was wearing a cream shirt tucked roughly into a pair of flannels that were held up by a thin leather belt.

'... I thought you'd hid it, didn't I?' Jack sounded as guilty as hell, even to himself.

What Parker did next was weird. Jack stared as he spread the raincoat out on the bed as if it was going to protect the top blanket from some horrible mess, one of the raincoat's arms hanging down like a dead man's. Jack's knees trembled on the thin bedside rug.

'A ball I hid in my chest – just in case you come up here to get it back?' Jack had never heard such a sneering voice.

''S'right. Sort of.'

'Sort of,' Parker repeated, quietly wheezing. 'Well, I'll tell you what I'm *sort of* gonna do myself.' He started pulling the thin leather belt from around his flannels. 'I'm gonna hand you over to her ladyship for sending back to the slums you come from. But first off I'm gonna give you a good Lambeth lickin', the sort we give to dogs who crap on our carpets, an' kids who thieve our precious pearls ...'

No! Help! Mum! The belt was out and Parker was winding one end of it around his right hand. And Jack was on his feet – he'd never got up off a floor so fast. But Parker was faster and shot out his belt hand to grab his neck, holding him in a tight, painful, poachers' grip. Jack kicked and shouted *'Help!'* just once at the top of his voice before Parker's long fingers came round to the front of his neck and pressed on his wind-pipe, choking him off.

'On that bed for the floggin' you're gonna get!'

'Aaargh!' Jack tried beating Parker with his fists, he kicked again at the man's legs, he bucked and bent, crouched and twisted, but he was held at arms' length and he couldn't get near him. Jack could do this all night and be held struggling here until he'd got no fight left in him. *And then he was going to get the worst sort of beatings going.* Now Parker started rolling up his sleeve, all the while smiling at Jack, and with a little shake of his head winking as if to say, 'Ain't we gonna enjoy this, sonny!'

And those scary words gave Jack a quick grab of London guile. He couldn't get at the man, but his hands were free and he could get at something – at the jug on the chest-of-drawers. Grabbing it up, he threw it at the man's head, a shot that missed, but which made him duck and bring his head down in front of him – which Jack kicked with all his force.

'Aaargh!'

Wearing only plimsolls, Jack's kick wasn't like a

good toeing from a coalman's boot, but it caught Parker on the nose, straight off starting his nose bleeding.

'You little – !'

With his neck now suddenly freed, Jack ran for the door and pulled it open. Parker was after him, but as he ran for the outside, Jack threw up his hand at the twin light switches – and instantly the stable-block was all lit-up. He jumped the stairs and landed awkwardly. He could hear Parker clattering down behind him, but somehow he got his balance back and sprinted for the house – to see the scullery door opening, and Clive waving his own torch, and to hear a shout from way upstairs where Florrie slept.

'Parker – put that light out! You want us all up in front of the beak?'

And within five minutes the house was alive, Parker getting first-aid from Florrie, and Jack, Clive and Wendy standing in the drawing room in front of Lady Ashwell in a furious, unforgiving mood.

'I have never been so disgusted and disappointed in all my life!' she said. 'Your explanations had better be on the far side of excellent!' With angry eyes she looked along the line; but Jack was dismayed to see that after she'd focused on each of them in turn her livid stare stayed mainly fixed on him.

Chapter Eighteen

It wasn't the magistrate Florrie called 'the beak' who was going to judge Jack, it was going to be the colonel. And the way it looked was bad. Jack had gone into Parker's room in the middle of the night, got caught with the chest-of-drawers open, and then jumped up and given the man a bloody nose. What Parker had been going to do to him didn't come into it – Lady Ashwell had just waved that part of the story away like a nasty smell. Plus, unfairest of all, Parker had driven to Dover that morning to bring the colonel home – with all that journey-time to get his side of things across.

When he got in from school Jack was told to change into his plimsolls and wait in his bedroom ready to be called down. He'd gone over everything with Clive. He and Wendy were in trouble, too – for being out of their beds and wearing daytime clothes in the night, and Lady Ashwell had got very cross with them when they wouldn't tell her why. But Parker had been in the room by then, holding a rag to his red nose – and who knew what he might have done if they'd told their mother about him being a spy – so they'd had to stick to the stupid lost ball story with Jack going to get it back. But it all ended up sounding as if they were just protecting him.

'So Jack curried favour by offering to get it back for you?'

'He was … just … being kind.'

Clive and Jack decided that what they'd say would

all depend on whether or not Parker was there when they were questioned by the colonel. If he was, they'd have to stick to their Wendy's ball story – the last thing they wanted was a German spy going berserk in the house, especially if the colonel wasn't carrying his pistol. But Jack made Clive promise to try to get his father to listen to him when Parker wasn't in the room. 'Else it's all just down to me, ain't it?'

'If only you'd found something in Parker's room!'

''Least I tried!' But his failure made Jack feel extra-guilty.

Within ten minutes he was called downstairs by Florrie. He found Clive and Wendy standing outside the drawing room door, their nervous faces turning his stomach over.

'Parker's in there,' Wendy whispered. 'Florrie's been in and she's come out very upset, but we don't know if he'll let Parker stay for us ...'

'Has your dad got his pistol?'

'Don't know. But he's in his uniform.'

The door suddenly opened and Parker came out. His nose was still red, stuck up in the air as if it might drop off, and looking to Jack as if it was a little bit more to one side of his face than the other, but he didn't dare stare for too long. The man gave him that sneering look again, which Jack took to mean that he'd just dropped him deep in the muck with Colonel Ashwell. But at least the man was out of the room and heading off to the stable-block.

'Jack! Come in!' the colonel shouted through the doorway.

Today he was a very different man from the one who'd raced Jack up the stairs and then whacked him with his pillow. The look on his face said he was just about ready to call out the firing squad. The drawing room looked scary, too. A table had been brought in, with the colonel sitting behind it, and Lady Ashwell at one side holding a pencil and a writing pad. An upright chair was in the middle of the room like a courtroom dock.

'Come in, boy, and sit down.'

Jack sat straight-backed on the chair and pushed his knees together, let his hands hang at his sides. He knew how to sit in the headmaster's office, you kept still, made no fuss, and said nothing to get him going until he got going of his own accord. You definitely didn't slouch. You were nine parts guilty anyway, so you didn't make it ten out of ten before he even started.

'Jack Bell, I had thought you were a decent type, a regular sort of fellow,' the colonel began. 'Men from all sorts of different backgrounds serve under me, and I always like to feel I know whom I can trust and whom I can't. The best soldier isn't necessarily the chap from the best home. Give me a rough diamond I can trust and I can fight to kingdom come.' He leant forward at Jack. 'So I ask myself, did I misjudge Boy Soldier Bell?'

'No, sir!' Jack replied smartly. Always speak up, mumbles sound as guilty as hell. And because Parker wasn't in here he didn't have to stick to that stupid ball story any more. He felt his shoulders begin to relax a little, and from the corner of his eye he saw Lady Ashwell writing something down, and he guessed it was what he'd just said. Well, just wait until he got going in a minute – she'd break her pencil lead. And when he told them that Clive and Wendy were in on the spy stuff he'd be well in the clear. He could definitely be one of those men who'd fight with the colonel to kingdom come.

'This story of yours about Wendy's, er, favourite ball ...' The colonel looked away from Jack and turned to Lady Ashwell. 'Did you have a favourite ball?' he asked her. 'Is it common among the girls?'

'I've got a favourite marble,' Jack put in. 'It's a Blood Orange with a blue – '

'Yes, well you need to know I don't believe a word of your ball story, young fellow. Got to tell you, I don't believe a deuced word.'

And this was just the moment Jack had been waiting for – to play his ace. 'An' nor don't I,' he said,'because I only said it to her while Parker was hanging about.'

'*Mister* Parker, please.'

'Mister Parker.'

'And are you referring to Lady Ashwell?'

'Yes, sir. It was an excuse. A get-out.'

'Good at get-outs, are you?' But Jack could see a trick question a mile off and he took a breath while he waited for the next question, the big one that was coming. *A cracking answer always sounds stronger after a question has been asked.*

'Then why *were* you up in the night, in Mr Parker's private quarters, rummaging through his personal effects – with my children supporting you back at base? Were they obeying your orders? Are they under your thrall?'

Jack didn't know where his thrall was so he couldn't answer that, but he could tell the colonel the mission he'd been on – and that he, Clive, and Wendy were all in this together; Woolwich kid or Lord Muck, he wasn't going to take the can back on his own.

'I said I'd do it,' he told the colonel.

'Was that a boast – or were you volunteering?'

Jack liked that word. 'Volunteering, sir.' He almost wanted to salute.

'To do what? For what purpose?'

Now for it.

'To find stuff in Mr Parker's quarters to prove what me an' Clive an' Wendy reckon …'

'"What all three of you reckon". Are you getting this down?' the colonel asked his wife.

'The bones, dear,' she said. 'The bones.'

'And what is it that you all *reckon?*' The colonel was still looking at his wife's swift-moving pencil, until Jack said it and the man's head suddenly spun back at him.

'We reckon Parker's a spy. A German spy. Like Mrs Rosewarn says there are, they're all over the place. He's come here years back pretending to be a Cockney, which he ain't – ' Jack stuck out his chest – 'an' he tucks himself up in London till the war starts, then he gets secret stuff off the English an' he sends it over to Germany.'

There. It was out – the real bones of it, after which Jack hardly drew breath. 'He's got diff'rent slang to proper cockneys, he's puttin' it on; an' he's your driver flappin' his ears at what's said, an' he carries that leather secrets case of secrets for you, an' he goes off in the night down to the farm, and he gets a secret flashlight signal tellin' him to go inside the barn …'

'Well, strop my razor!' The colonel was standing up now. 'I've never heard such hokum in all my life!'

'Ridiculous!' Lady Ashwell joined in, waiting until that moment to break her pencil-lead. 'Just a lot of cheap-jack fiction.'

Jack stared from one to the other. They were still blaming him, as if it was him who'd started it all off, a naughty London boy spoiling their little darlings, some toe-rag from the back end of Woolwich. He was angry, his eyes hurt with the heat of it, and any second his chest was going to burst up out of his mouth filled with a string of words saying just what he thought of them. But an instant before that could happen the drawing room door suddenly burst open. He jumped. Everyone turned. Who was it – Parker with a tommy gun?

It was Wendy. She came in holding something behind her back and ran to the table, followed through the door by Clive. 'I think you should look at this, Da.'

'Wen, have you been ear-wigging?'

'Of course I have. We both have. To make sure all this is fair.'

'*Fair?*' For a second or so the colonel looked as if he would bluster but he didn't. He put out his hand to be given whatever it was Wendy was holding behind her back. But Jack already knew what it was; he'd known what it was before he saw it: it was the red notebook they'd found hidden under Parker's room.

'We found this the other day, tucked above the sink in the stable-block. Parker must have put it there.'

The colonel came from behind the table and took the notebook from her. He flipped through it, frowning. 'Like a tradesman's, or a bookie's runner's …' He showed it to Lady Ashwell.

'It's certainly Parker's calligraphy,' she said. 'But it's not in a Germanic form.'

'Well, it wouldn't be if he were a half-decent spy, would it?' the colonel remarked.

Jack's inside did a little dance. The man was taking this seriously, not throwing it out through the back door like old suds. Wendy turned and smiled at him, and Clive said. 'Spiffo!'

But the colonel made a noise in his throat like a car being cranked. 'What a load of old tosh! What a bucketful of bally nonsense! Parker mustn't hear a word of this. He'll up and leave, and good men are deuced hard to get in wartime. We'll stick with Wendy's ball, thank you very much, ridiculous as it is.' He dropped a shoulder, seemed to relax a little. 'I don't mind a bit of a josh. A spot of larking-about keeps the Tommy on his toes. But this is really is arrant nonsense!' He turned to look at Lady Ashwell, folded his arms and gave a sardonic laugh. 'Dear, oh dear, oh dear. What *has* Adolf Hitler done to us all?'

Jack's insides stopped dancing as he realised that Colonel Ashwell had turned to face him as he said it. Him, not Wendy, and not Clive. *Him.*

'What had Adolf Hitler *and Jack Bell* done to them all?' That was what he'd really said.

Chapter Nineteen

For a while Jack felt at odds with the other two. They were family, and he wasn't. He hadn't found anything in Parker's room, and now they seemed OK about giving up on Parker being a spy. They wound up the wires between the bedrooms and put the dynamos back onto their bikes. But Jack had never been one to brood. He was a move-on sort of kid. If he couldn't wangle himself in at the Odeon he'd go across to the Granada; and if he couldn't get in there he'd go to the Globe flea-pit pictures. What he never did was nothing. And now, with the others turning their backs on Parker spy stuff he could think hard over what to do about someone else. Shirley Filer.

She'd been in a worse state at school that day than she'd ever been. Betts and Bennett hadn't look so hot, either, but he wasn't worried about them. Shirley had a big red mark on the side of her face which she tried to cover with her hand. She always looked drippy, but now she looked scared – really scared. Her eyes were swollen and stared like a skeleton's; and when a desk lid cracked shut she nearly hit the rafters. Doing her work, she just held her head in her hand and looked down at her exercise book – and from the cack-handed way she was holding her pencil her knuckles had to be as raw as if she'd had a stick across them. He had never felt sorry for Shirley before – always whining around Depot Street like a cat nobody ever stroked – but today had been different. With her living upstairs from them and their mothers being best friends, he had to think of her as sort-of family – and if all the Ashwells could stick together, then so could the Bells and the Filers.

'You all right, Shirl? You want me to tell Miss?'

'No! You shut it!' But she was shaking. 'You keep your nose out!' And when he looked at it closely her own nose was as puffy as a punchy's.

So Jack kept out of things – for then. But now he was definitely going to do something. He was going to send that postcard home to his mother, get her to tell Ivy upstairs she'd got to come down here and take Shirley back home. Never mind air raids – the girl couldn't look much worse if a German bomb blew her over the coal yard.

Parker and the car were away when Jack and Clive came in from school. He was driving the colonel back to Dover. But they were met by Wendy, keeping watch for them.

'Come into the dining room!' she said. 'Ma's waiting for you, to do a code.'

'Morse, or semaphore?' Clive asked, showing a semaphore 'U' with wide arms.

That sounded good to Jack.

'On paper,' Wendy said, 'letters.'

As he walked into the dining room things felt a bit different. Lady Ashwell didn't give him a black look, and she'd put a chair for him with the others she'd set around the table.

'While Mr Parker's away Wendy has put the red notebook back where you found it,' she told Jack and Clive. 'But I've copied out the pages and Wendy's going to lead us in breaking the code.'

'Spiffo!' Clive said. 'Why? Do you think he *could* be a spy?'

'Not for an instant,' his mother snapped with a look at Jack. 'Do you think Da's stupid? The man drives a military vehicle for him, do you think he wouldn't have had the most rigorous of checks done?'

'So why're you doing this?' Jack asked – which seemed a fair question.

'Because Wendy's missed a lot of school this term, and codes are words and they are logic. Brain food. But it won't hurt the two of you to watch while she works through it.'

'Ma wants to know what old Parker's up to.' Wendy's eyes were bright. 'A few lady friends back in London? He does like his day-off trains.'

'I don't like mysteries, and that notebook is a mystery. Now – ' Lady Ashwell clapped her hands at the others seated at the table.

'We look like a committee,' Wendy said.

'With some decisions to make. But if any of you were to breathe a word …'

'Guides' honour.' Wendy stood and saluted.

'Cross my heart and wish to die,' Clive crossed his heart and slit his throat.

'On me mother's death bed,' said Jack, bowing too low and cracking his head on the table.

'Unnecessary, Jack. Now – ' Lady Ashwell pushed the copied code in front of Wendy, where Clive and Jack could lean over and see it. It was on a sheet of letter-writing notepaper. 'On his first page we have this …' She pointed to the line of numbers along the top. They ran *8 11 24 19 21 20 25 11 31*. Underneath them was another line of numbers running *29 21 18 25 11 18 11 31 25 26 24 11 11 26 – 19 7 26 26 14 11 29 25*, with a cross at the end of it like a sum that was wrong. 'Now – ' Lady Ashwell whisked the paper away and in its place she put a book with a bookmark in it – *Nicholas Nickleby* by Charles Dickens. She opened it and pointed to the chapter description at the top of chapter three.

MR RALPH NICKLEBY RECEIVES SAD TIDINGS OF HIS BROTHER, BUT BEARS UP NOBLY AGAINST THE INTELLIGENCE COMMUNICATED TO HIM.

'Now, take your time, Wen, and using this sheet of paper – ' Lady Ashwell tore off a clean sheet from her writing pad – 'I should like you to note down the number of times each letter makes its appearance in the extract. Count them, and take your time.' She sat back – and so did he. Wendy could do the hard work.

He watched as she wrote out the alphabet and started counting, beginning with 'A'. Against each letter she wrote the number of times it was printed in the extract, from no times for 'F', 'J', 'Q', 'W', 'X' and 'Z' to ten each for 'E' and 'I'.

'Now, what have you got? Which letter or letters appear most frequently?'

'"E" and "I",' Wendy said.

'"E" and "I",' Lady Ashwell repeated.

'"E, I addy-oh, the farmer's in his den!"' sang Jack.

'Now, it's an established fact that the most frequently employed letter in the English language is "E". So, going though these jottings of Parker's – ' Lady Ashwell took the book away and replaced it with the copied-out code. 'Which number appears most times?'

Wendy went down the sheet. But what if Parker was a spy after all and this was all in German? That'd upset the apple cart, wouldn't it?

'Number eleven,' Wendy said.

'Which could mean that number eleven represents the letter "E" or the letter "I". So, let's go first with "E". Assuming that he wouldn't simply leave "E" as number five in the alphabet, if it's eleven, what would twenty-nine be?' Lady Ashwell pointed to the first number in the top line of the code.

Wendy and Clive pored over the paper. '"W",' said Clive and Wendy together. Jack blew blow his nose; he'd worked out a long time before that no one expects an answer from a boy who's busy with his rag and his nose.

'So, can we make any sense if we fill in the other numbers with letters based on eleven being "E"?'

'They'd all be six letters on,' said Clive, and Wendy started working it out. 'This is fun,' he said.

Prrrrark went Jack's nose into his handkerchief.

The two of them soon had it all worked out. The number eleven for the letter 'E' seemed to fit, so they weren't even asked to do anything about the letter 'I', and Wendy wrote out the three pages of notes, one under the other.

The pages read, 'BERMONDSEY WOLSELEY STREET – MATTHEWS; DENMARK HILL – DEWHURST; CAMBERWELL NEW ROAD – STENT AND LINTORN.'

'A fairly simple code for a fairly simple man,' Lady Ashwell said, 'but what I'm asking myself is what does it mean? I can discern addresses, yes, in the sense of Bermondsey, Lambeth, and Deptford being London boroughs with street names – but who is "Matthews", and who is "Dewhurst", and who are "Stent and Lintorn" – are they personal contacts of some sort?'

'Ladies' married names?' Wendy suggested.

'Bookies' runners?' Clive said. 'Like Da said.'

Jack stuffed his handkerchief deep into his trousers pocket, and put up his hand as if he was in class. 'I know what they are!' he said, stretching his neck to breaking.

'Go on.' The three of them were waiting for him.

'Easy. They're all round our way, up London – Matthews's, Dewhurst's, and Stentsy's ...'

'What are they?' Clive wanted to know. 'Shops of some sort?'

Jack turned to him, drew out what he'd got to say slowly to make it sound clever. 'Butchers, aren't they? Butchers' shops. Matthews in New Road, an' Dewhurst in Artillery Place; an' my mum goes to the market most times, but she always gets Christmas stuff down Stentsy's in Clara Place.'

'Butchers ...' Lady Ashwell mused, and went on repeating the word, frowning to herself. 'Butchers, butchers, butchers ...'

'And the farm!' Clive shouted. 'The farm! Butchers, and Parker going to the farm!'

Now everyone's back was scout-pole straight.

'Well, well, well,' said Lady Ashwell. And she went on saying it until the well was dry. 'Well, well, well, well, well ...'

Jack tried to keep a clever look on his face; he'd hit on something, that was definite, he'd sorted out some mystery – but he was jiggered if he knew what it was he'd done.

'Well, well, well, well, well ...'

Anyway, before he was found out not knowing, he'd got something else to do today so he left it at that. He got up politely and went to his room to rummage in his case for the evacuation postcard his mother had given him. *The* card. He dug out the pencil she'd put in with it, and balancing the suitcase across his knees he sat on the bed and wrote her a message.

'Dear Mum. Im allright but shirlys' bad, beat up and ill. Get ivy doun to tak her home or shill be ded. Love Jack.'

The card was already stamped, he'd told Bennett a lie, so now he had to get it to the post-box that was cemented in the street wall of the school. He wanted this to go tonight. Running downstairs he bumped into Wendy.

'Can I lend your bike, Wen? Please?'

'No, but you can borrow it.'

She went with him to the shed where they wheeled it out. But before she let him get onto it, with one hand on the saddle and the other on the handlebars she leant through the bike frame and suddenly kissed him on the cheek – the surprise of it making him drop the post-card on the ground.

'I think you're very brave,' she said, 'doing the looking in Parker's room. I didn't want to go, and – ' she dropped her voice – 'neither did Clive.'

'Nor did I. An' you won't wanna know what Parker was goin' to do to me if I hadn't slung that jug at him ...'

'Clive told me.'

160

They both shuddered at the thought, but Jack's was partly a frisk of pleasure at what she'd just done. She'd kissed him – and gone red after. She quickly bent down and picked up the postcard, giving it back to him with a quick look first, but he couldn't dwell for long on her reading it. He didn't have a bike of his own and he rarely got to ride one; and Wendy's saddle was a bit high for him, so he had to pretend his foot had slipped off the pedal when he fell off the first time, and he blamed the handlebars for being wonky when he fell off the second. But he finally got his balance and cycled off down the driveway – carrying down inside his shirt his call for help for the girl upstairs, poor old Shirley Filer.

Chapter Twenty

Jack's legs were twitching for afternoon play when Lady Ashwell walked into the school hall.

'Is Miss Buckshoot in her old classroom?' she asked Mrs Rosewarn.

'Yes, through there.' Mrs Rosewarn went on marking Debra Pagett's English book. 'Is this a "b" or a "d"?' She was just the same back at Union Street when the headmaster walked in. Lady Ashwell went on through – and Jack looked across at Clive. *What was this?* Was there still going to be a come-uppance from that fight between Clive and Bennett? But, no – in a few moments Miss Buckshoot brought Lady Ashwell back, and, without asking Mrs Rosewarn's permission, she called out to the class from the front.

'Shirley Filer?' Everyone turned to Shirley, who put her head on her desktop and covered it with her arms. 'Will you come with us, please?'

Shirley didn't move – so Miss Buckshoot wriggled her out of her desk. Grumbling under her breath, Shirley stood in the aisle at the side. Jack knew she'd hate him for sending the postcard so he hadn't told her, but she gave him a look across the hall that said 'Traitor' – about the most alive he'd seen her since they'd come here. Anyway, this didn't have to be to do with that, did it? It could be Lady Ashwell checking up on something about the farm. But he knew he'd been right to post that card. Shirley looked worse every day, and now she'd got a scurvy rash around her mouth.

'We'll talk in my room,' Miss Buckshoot told her, leading her by the arm as she called across to Mrs Rosewarn. 'Would you kindly cover playtime for me?' Mrs Rosewarn looked very definitely as if she'd kindly rather not, but she sent Debra Pagett back to her seat and sat the class up ready to go out, while Miss Buckshoot took Lady Ashwell and Shirley to the small office just inside the school door.

'What's all that about?' Clive asked Jack. 'What's Ma up to?'

Jack said nothing about the postcard, but he was starting to put a couple of things together in his head. 'Could be she's checking on the farm,' he said. 'About the code.'

'Excellent, Musketeer. She doesn't like a mystery, the Ma.'

But Jack couldn't go along with giving Lady A any pats on the back until he knew she wasn't making things worse for Shirley. ''Long as she don't use her like a, you know …'

'A witness?'

'Yeah.' Jack knew how tell-tale-tits always ended up crying louder than kids who kept their mouths shut.

'She'll know how to do it fairly,' Clive said. 'But that girl couldn't look any worse if she'd been chased by Charlie the bull.' And that was true, Jack thought. But if what he'd done ended up getting her hurt some more then he'd have failed all round – not proved that Parker was a spy and not helped Shirley Filer.

She didn't return to Mrs Rosewarn's class after play. Lady Ashwell seemed to have gone and Miss

Buckshoot was back in her classroom with her own children, the only other place Shirley could be. But those kids were younger – and why would she be put in there? She didn't need saving from Mrs Rosewarn's class, she wasn't being bullied and beaten-up by anyone at school.

Mrs Rosewarn kept everyone's head down with *A Year With Nature*, reading round the class about seed dispersal, and she ended the afternoon with the next instalment of *The Water-Babies*, which she read perching on her desk as if it was a treat. But when the bell was rung there was still no sign of Shirley, and Jack walked home with Clive, nothing much to say, telling himself that Ivy Filer couldn't have got down here as quickly as that, could she?

When Jack and Clive walked into the kitchen it wasn't Ivy Filer sitting at the table sipping at a mug of milk, it was Shirley.

'Well, I'll be blowed! What you doin' here?' Jack didn't ask unkindly, he almost put a hand on her shoulder.

'Lady brung me.'

Florrie poured milk for Jack and Clive. 'She's staying here pro-tem, got the room next to me. We're gonna be mates, ain't we, girlie?'

Shirley shrugged.

'Any cakies about?' Clive asked.

'With me ironing sheets and making beds? You'll be wanting me to do you a dance next.' Florrie stuck out her lower lip and blew at a wisp of hair she didn't have. 'And you can all watch your p's an' q's 'cos the colonel's coming back special for a couple of hours.'

Lady Ashwell came into the kitchen. 'Excellent.' But Jack couldn't think what was excellent – except for Shirley being got away from the farm. The colonel was coming back, which probably meant another load of stuff going on in the front room.

'Jack, well done for sending that postcard home,' Lady Ashwell said. 'Your mother alerted Mrs Filer, and then she alerted me, by telephone.' Jack pulled a face; he couldn't imagine his mother using a telephone; she always said she didn't know button 'B' from a kick up the bum. 'She sends you her love.' She bowed at Jack as if it was her giving it. 'I spoke to Edith Lewis and she suggested this change, if we had room.'

'Which we have,' said Florrie.

Shirley finished her milk and laid the mug on the table as if it was best china. Something about her made Jack take a harder look at her face. Already her eyes were less puffy, and she had Vaseline around her sore mouth – with a couple of crumbs in it, so someone had had some cake.

'Shirley is upstairs next to Florrie, and she'll change into one of Wendy's dresses – she's looking a few things out – and you boys are to put on your house shoes and stay indoors, no getting hot.' Lady Ashwell spoke specifically to Clive. 'Da's coming home for an hour or so, and I want the house quiet, so you can organise a game of "Sorry" in the dining room ...'

'Is he posted?' Clive asked.

'You know we never discuss his movements.'

'But the car's outside the stable-block, Parker's cleaning it, and it's an hour to Dover and an hour back ...'

Jack knew full well where Parker and the car were. He kept a weather eye open for the man because he knew darned well what he'd get if he ever got caught on his own – with Lady Ashwell being told some trumped-up story about what he'd done to deserve it.

'Da's on his way. You can have an after-school wash, and then keep yourselves clean and quiet.' This was for Clive and Jack. She turned to Shirley – 'And Shirley, you'll change and lie on your bed for an hour or so while we conduct some family business. But hold yourself ready, in case the colonel calls you down.'

Shirley's face said she didn't know what the devil was going on – but then it wasn't very often she did. Jack had an idea what this was all about, though. If the colonel might want to speak to her, it had to be to do with the farm – what she'd seen, what she knew – so it was a cert this was mixed up with Parker and the notebook code. And that would be why Parker hadn't gone to Dover in the car to fetch the colonel. A shiver ran through him. One way or another, in a little while it was all going to be a bit tasty around here …

The colonel arrived on the pillion of an army motorcycle, in uniform, cocking his leg over to get off and giving a curt command to the army rider to take himself round to the kitchen for 'a cup of char and a bun'. He strode into the house, kissed Lady Ashwell and Wendy, offered a handshake to Clive and nodded to Jack, before leading his wife into the drawing room, where Florrie took tea – and came back wearing a mournful face.

'He's going away,' she whispered, keeping her voice down from the soldier outside the kitchen door. 'France.'

Clive and Wendy looked at one another. Wendy stood up as if to look brave, and Clive said, 'Good old Da. He'll soon sort out the Jerries.' He turned to Jack. 'He can be our third Musketeer, on the foreign field. "One for all, and all for one".'

Jack nodded, he supposed the colonel could. But it was hard to get choked up about their father. He hadn't got one of his own and he'd never had one, it didn't hit him one way or the other about fathers going off.

The man himself suddenly re-appeared in the doorway and went through to where his motorcycle rider was perched on a chair at the top of the cellar steps holding a mug of tea and smoking a cigarette. The soldier stood up smartly and snuffed his Woodbine. 'Reynolds, be so good as to go across to the stable-block and tell Mr Parker that I should like to see him in the drawing room. Straight away.'

'Yes, sir.'

'Accompany him back and bring him through, then keep a presence outside the door.'

'Right you are, sir.' The soldier went off across the courtyard. 'And the three of you, into the dining room with a board game.'

'Yes, Da.'

'Do it now. Before Parker comes across.'

Jack shivered. Parker was coming over; but at least there were others about, and the man was being treated like someone up in court, with a guard. An excited scare rolled his stomach. This was deadly serious stuff.

Abruptly, the colonel went back to the drawing room. He was still in his uniform but without his cap; and, as far as Jack could see, neither did he have his pistol in its holster.

'Come on. I'll get the "Sorry".' Wendy scooted off upstairs, and was quickly back in the dining room, where Clive was putting three chairs at one end of the table.

'Lay it out,' he told Wendy. 'Set it up as if we're playing. I'll be red, Jack can be blue, and you can be yellow.'

Jack frowned. 'I dunno how to play. I know Ludo. 'Aven't you got Ludo?'

'This is more fun,' Wendy told him. 'No one wins till the last minute. And you can be *vicious*! Worse than croquet.' She started setting out the pieces. 'You'll pick it up as we go along.'

'Don't worry about "Sorry",' Clive told him, 'we're not actually going to play.' He lowered his voice. 'We're going to listen.' He pointed to the wall dividing this room from the drawing room. 'I'll get the glasses.'

'*Glasses?*' Jack asked. 'You got magic ones that see through bloomin' walls?' His face said pull-the-other-leg.

'*Drinking* glasses,' Clive told him, going to the sideboard and taking out three crystal tumblers. 'Once Parker's in there, we listen, like when you were in there.' Jack still didn't understand, but old Clive usually knew what he was doing. And at that moment the three of them were caught like a snapshot as a voice came from outside in the hallway.

'You go in,' the motorcycle soldier said. 'I'll wait for you out here.'

'Dunno what all this stuff an' nonsense is about,' Jack heard Parker say. 'I can't be dragooned to going abroad. My asthma ...' A loud, throaty cough underlined his unfitness for active service.

'Soon find out, won't you?' the soldier said – and the drawing room door closed firmly.

'And so shall we,' Clive said. He gave Wendy and Jack a glass each and went across to the party wall. 'Ssssh.' With a finger to his lips he put the open end of his glass to the wall and pressed an ear against its base. Now Jack understood. Quickly, he went across and did the same, and the three of them jostled for space in the gap between the sideboard and the drinks cabinet. Like Clive and Wendy he put his glass between the wall and his ear, and he smiled as he realised how clearly he could hear the voices from the other room. This had to be like the school doctor listening to chests, or the King talking on the wireless.

'Code?' he heard Parker saying. 'What code, sir? What would I be doing with a code?'

'This is your notebook, isn't it?' It was Lady Ashwell's voice. 'You've agreed that this is your red notebook, kept in the garage?'

'Yes, ma'am, for parts for the Morris. Running repairs. I like to keep the motor up to scratch, never know when there's going to be an emergency.'

'In Bermondsey and Denmark Hill and Camberwell?' she went on.

'Dealers, Ma'am, handy places for picking up spares, a bit cheaper than the big boys. It's all for the colonel, Ma'am.'

'*Dealers*, you say?' the colonel asked. 'Motor-car dealers, is that it?'

'Spares dealers, sir. Small-time. Not vehicles.'

Jack pressed even harder with his glass. They were getting to the bottom of what that Parker stuff was all about; and now he was listening for the word he knew was coming next.

'Motor-car spares dealers in three London districts – at the back end of *butchers'* shops?'

The quietness was filled with the sound of breathing on this side of the wall. Then, '*Butchers'* shops?' Parker repeated. 'God bless my soul, no ...' He started coughing and wheezing.

'God bless it, indeed – because I'll tell you what you're up to,' the colonel went on.

Jack looked at the others as he waited to hear what the colonel had decided Parker was up to. The sound of the silence in the drawing room was so clear through the glass that Jack could almost see the colonel standing in there like a man in a wig in a murder film.

'In the middle of 1917, towards the end of the Great War, Britain was forced to introduce food rationing. On a limited scale. Foodstuffs from abroad were having difficulty getting through, expensive both in ships sunk and men's lives sacrificed, and there was a danger of the country running out of certain commodities. As a result we had ration cards issued, restricting us to certain amounts of certain foods per month, no matter what anyone might be able to afford ...'

'Well, we all remember some of that,' Parker said – without any 'sir' or 'ma'am' this time; Jack could hear how his tone had changed, like a kid who's going to get stroppy before he got the stick.

'... And I'll tell you what we've got in this notebook here, Parker. We've got the names of several butchers' shops that you've visited on your days off in London, with indications in the form of a tick or a cross as to the likelihood of a dishonest butcher being prepared to buy off-ration meat if food rationing comes in again – as it will.'

'What a load of – ' Parker began.

'And we have it on good evidence that you have been making late-night rendezvous with the Hundens at the farm, no doubt setting up some scheme or other for providing that meat ...'

Jack's glass nearly slipped from his sweaty fingers. *This was where their middle-of-the-night tracking bit was coming in!* Any minute now and they could be called next door to stand up and swear on the Bible to tell the truth.

'That's a load of tosh!' Parker said. 'If I go down the farm in my own time that's my business ...'

'*Dishonest* business,' the colonel said. 'You were let into the barn after a signal from a flashlight. There are witnesses to it.'

Jack suddenly wanted to go to the lavatory, seriously.

'There's nothing dishonest about a bit o' courting,' Parker sneered. 'I go down there to see Eva, she's my girl. I go in the night – but I've never been too tired to do my duties and my driving. You can't lay that on me.'

'Why that late?'

'Her folks don't fancy me, bein' older ...'

'Is that the truth, Parker?' Lady Ashwell's voice came in.

'It is, ma'am.'

There was another longish wait. Wendy, Clive, and Jack looked at each other with eyes that didn't blink; no one dared speak for fear they'd miss the next vital thing to come through the wall.

'Well, I'm afraid it isn't the truth Parker, not entirely,' the colonel went on. 'Perhaps your … *romance* is … but after her ladyship's telephone call to me I made a few calls of my own, to some of these London butchers, those with a declining cross against their names in your notebook. And I have had it confirmed to me that they have recently been approached by a person answering your description who was offering extra cuts of meat in the event of rationing coming in …'

'Oh!' This was a high and sudden shout from Lady Ashwell. 'Oh! You despicable creature!' Jack heard a chair going over.

'Sylvia …'

'Would you like to know, Parker, although I doubt that you would, that while people like you were making their dishonest money towards the end of the Great War, fine men like my father – not *like* my father, including my father *himself* – were losing their lives at Arras and Passchendaele. They were giving their lives so that your sort of creature could thrive in a colony of rats!' She suddenly sounded like a girl to Jack, not a Lady; she was like the person inside herself, the one without the toffee round the apple. 'He goes, Johnnie! He goes. I'm not prepared to stay in a house in any sort of proximity to a man like this!'

'And you'd be right, Sylvia.'

A long wheeze from Parker turned into a shout. 'You've got no proof, an' even if what you're saying was right, I've not done anything yet, have I? So you can't get me on anything!'

'Which is the only reason there won't be any police charges. But your employment here is at an end. You'll be paid up to the end of the month – which is a deal more generous than you deserve, and you will leave first thing tomorrow. You pack up, and you go, without a reference – to your lady friend, or back to your London haunts. But Ashwell Hall is closed to you from tomorrow morning onwards.'

Movement could be heard from the other side of the wall. On Jack's side of it there was a panic nip to the sideboard with the crystal glasses, and a dash to the table where in no time Jack, Clive, and Wendy had their heads bent over the 'Sorry' board, pretending to play. They heard Parker go out of the drawing room with a slam of its door. 'Steady!' the soldier said. Footsteps moved off across the hallway floor, and the dining room door opened a crack. Lady Ashwell looked in at the innocent scene.

'I think I win,' Wendy said, pretending to move a yellow piece into a square marked 'Home'.

'I reckon we all win,' said Jack, very softly under his breath.

Chapter Twenty-one

'Well done you three,' the colonel said. 'But another time you alert the adults when you suspect something's not up to snuff. A man like that could have turned nasty ...'

He did, Jack thought. *Blooming nasty!*

'Anyway, Reynolds and I will stay the night – Florrie can make him up a camp bed beside the car. We shan't want any sabotage.'

They were all in the dining room where Florrie had served 'high tea', sausages with spaghetti-in-tomato-sauce, the sort of meal Jack enjoyed. Shirley was given a seat next to him, and she did look different, wearing Wendy's clothes and with her hair brushed.

The colonel was in a regimental rugby shirt, into which he had tucked his napkin as if he were dining in the officers' mess. But him looking casual still didn't get much talk going, no one seemed to know what it was safe to talk about: Jack and the others couldn't let on that they'd heard everything through the wall; and Lady Ashwell was looking down the table as if she was dreading telling her children that their father was soon going to France.

But Jack wasn't one for sitting in silence, and when all the polite serving and the passing of the salt, pepper, and sauce was done, he broke it. 'We thought they was spies at the farm,' he said. 'Because of them being called Hunden.' That stopped a couple of forks on the way to people's mouths.

'Why's that, Jack?' the colonel asked.

'Well, Hunden … like, it's got "hun" in it.'

The colonel laughed as if it was the ripest joke he'd heard in years. 'So the king's a bowl of soup because he's called "Windsor", is he?' Clive cracked up at that, but Jack didn't get it until it was explained.

'But he didn't say the proper words for a Cockney …'

'Who would that be?' Lady Ashwell asked.

'Parker. Mr Parker. Like, where I come from we say "Chathams" for socks – "Chatham docks". He says "Tilbury's", he's sort of made it up.' He took another largish mouthful; second helpings only ever went onto empty plates.

The colonel rested his cutlery and shook his head. 'Most slang is local. In the army it varies from regiment to regiment for exactly the same item. One man calls his gaiters "gaiters" and the next man calls them his "puttees". And your slang, Jack, Cockney rhyming slang – well, you can have whatever you want. If a man's from south London he might say "Chathams", Kent, but if he's from the east side he might say "Tilburys", which is Essex. And it can change by the day.'

'Oh.'

'People pick up things from each other.' The colonel nodded towards Clive. 'Clive says "spiffo" rather a lot, a little too much …' Well, Jack knew he'd copied that himself. '… And I've heard him come out with a couple of "wotchas".'

'Definitely too many,' Lady Ashwell threw in.

'Exchange,' the colonel said. 'Social interaction of words and of character, too.' That had everyone frowning. 'For example, I think Clive has learned some London guts from Jack here, leading an expedition out in the middle of the night – and Jack has learned some table manners.'

Jack slid the spaghetti off his knife. 'No, I ain't having that,' he heard himself saying. 'He's got all the guts in the world, Clive. He took on Bennett for me, and no one ever wants to do that.' He pointed his fork at the colonel. 'You could definitely take him fighting to Kingdom Come.'

'Not talking like a common soldier, though,' Lady Ashwell said.

'Although common soldiers are the ones who do most of the dying,' Wendy said.

The atmosphere was definitely awkward now; and Lady Ashwell did something about it. 'Anyway, we're delighted to have Shirley at table with us, and I think we should welcome her with a treat. Do you like ginger beer?' she asked her. Shirley nodded her head. 'So I think we shall crack open a bottle.'

'Spiffo!' said Clive.

'Jack – you're one of the family now, you shall fetch it for us.'

'Right-ho.' Jack straightened up. *One of the family!*

'From the cellar. The "refuge room". There are a couple of bottles on the shelf, bring one up, it'll be nice and cold from down there. We can replace it tomorrow. Pop and get one, would you?'

'Ginger pop!'

But Jack didn't get quite the laugh he thought he deserved because the colonel trumped him with, 'Down the apples and pairs you go! Hah!'

Jack left the dining room and went through the

kitchen to the cellar door. He only had one back door at home, but here there were two, one going out of the kitchen, then another one going to the outside, what Florrie called the scullery door. Between them was the door down to the cellar. Cautiously, he went down its steep steps, with just enough light from the scullery for him to see his way. Facing him now was the door into the cellar itself.

It was colder down here, and he shivered. He'd only been down here that one time when the air raid siren had gone, but he remembered seeing the bottles on their shelf, so he knew where he had to go when he went through the door. It wasn't locked; he pushed it open, which swung on oiled hinges and hit the inside wall with a crack that made him jump. Now he had to find the light switch because it was spooky dark in here. He fumbled around the wall to his right, but he couldn't locate it. He tried to his left, behind the open door, but that wouldn't be where it was, it was the wrong side. He decided it had to be at the bottom of the stairs, so it could be switched on before you came in. He turned to go out again – and then he heard it. *Oh, my God!* His body went into shock, like volts running through him from his feet up to his head. What he could hear paralysed him – the sound of wheezing in the pitch dark. *The sound of Parker.*

'Well, well, well!' The door closed with a bang, with Jack still inside. 'Well, I never did!' No voice had ever sounded so scary. It wasn't angry, it wasn't loud, it wasn't high and it wasn't low. It was very flat. 'Got you now, 'aven't I?' Jack couldn't speak; his jaw seemed to be wired up. 'An' me with nothing to lose. Your word against mine. An' you'll have so many teeth down your throat it'll be three weeks before you can whistle Dixey, let alone rat on me.'

Jack could just about see the shape of the man, standing a yard away, with the glint of something at his side that could have been a bottle of whisky, which he stooped to put on the floor.

'Get off! Get away from me! *Help!*' But Jack knew it was useless, he wouldn't be heard from down here. Everyone was miles away in the dining room, and Florrie had gone back upstairs. What could he do? Go for Parker first, take a kick at his privates, jump up at his head and try to screw it off? But the man was big, he loomed there like a meaty coalman. It would take two kids to stand even a chance against him, and Clive was nowhere near. *Mum!* Why couldn't they have been sent down here together?

Parker wheezed again. 'Now then,' he said, 'I'm gonna enjoy this. It's gonna send me on my way laughing.'

Clive! If only Clive was here. Two against Parker would be better than one. Clive could kick, he could scrag – or one of them could run for help. But Clive wasn't here!

Jack stared at Parker coming towards him.

No, but what would Clive do? He came out with all sorts of good ideas. *What would he do right now?*

'Now let's see what Woolwich boys are made of!' Parker moved the bottle further out of his way.

Clive's dad! The 'Da'. Clive would use his dad. Jack could hear how he'd do it. He'd come over all bossy as the boy from Ashwell Hall and he'd threaten Parker with the colonel. He'd let Parker know that

178

if he did anything to him, he was going to get tons worse back. But the colonel wasn't Jack's dad, he wouldn't care so much about what his evacuee said; and Parker would know that.

But he could still do the same sort of thing, couldn't he? Why couldn't Jack Bell could have a father, too?

He took in a deep breath to make himself sound cocky and full of blow. He lifted his head in an imitation of Clive being a soldier, a Musketeeer. 'If you bash me up, Mr Parker, you ain't gonna like what happens ...'

'I'm gonna like it very much, Toe-rag.'

'... 'An I'll tell you for why. My dad – '

'Your dad? Has a little basket like you got a dad?' Parker laughed, ending up wheezing, but merrily.

'I've got a dad all right, an' you've seen him. Over Dover, not far off. Sergeant Bell ...'

'Sergeant Bell?'

'That big man on the gate.' Jack knew all about the Royal Artillery barracks at Woolwich, where the Military Police with armbands guarded the way in and out. There was one man up there called 'the gorilla' who scruffed any kids away who tried to sell bits to the squaddies, and made any girls hanging around sling their hooks. He was a giant of a man – and they had to have blokes like him at all the army gates, especially with a war on.

Now he was going to be Jack's dad.

'He won't let you off light like the colonel. He'll come looking for you wherever you go. He knows London, he knows pubs, an' dog tracks, an' back streets. He'll find you – an' you won't just be left with your teeth down your throat, you'll be left floatin' arse-up in the river.'

'Don't give me that! That's a load of cock an' bull.' But Parker suddenly didn't sound so sure.

'It's a load o' truth. Why d'you think Lady A was sent to the village hall special for me, why was they holding me back? Eh?'

Parker said nothing.

''Cos of my dad. He told the colonel. Asked him to get me.'

'Your dad?' Parker sneered, but at least he'd stopped making a move for Jack – for a few moments.

'Now get out me way. Where's that light?' Jack tried to keep up the Clive voice, all in charge, all officer stuff – although his inside was churning. All he'd done was hold off a welting and a kicking for a second or two.

'Jack?'

The voice came like the sound of an angel direct from heaven; Clive's voice, calling down the cellar steps.

'Have you got lost – or are you guzzling all the fizzy?'

Parker swore and backed off into the darkness, and Jack turned to the door, just as it opened from the other side.

'You in here, Jack? Why didn't you put the light on?' As the cellar lit up, Clive's head came round the woodwork.

'Couldn't find it, could I?'

'Aha!' Clive came in, and went across to take a bottle of ginger beer from the shelf. There was no sign of Parker, he had to be behind the curtain that hung across the lavatory space. 'We're all parched up there. Couldn't spit a sixpence.'

Clive led the way back up the stairs, and Jack turned off the light for him. He had decided to leave Parker where he was. If Parker was forced to tell the Jack's dad story, he'd be told the truth – and weak as it might be, Jack wanted the man to think with just a little chink of his brain that Jack really did have a big, strong, dad like that.

And for the first time in his life, he sort of wanted it for himself.

Chapter Twenty-two

Ivy Filer came down on the Saturday. Jack guessed she would. He wondered if his mother might come down to keep her company, and perhaps to take him home. From what they head on the wireless, things were all very quiet in London; no bombs had been dropped, and people were having to be told to still carry their gas masks. But she didn't. Ivy just turned up out of the blue and rang the doorbell, all hot and bothered because it was a long walk from the bus stop up the drive to the Hall.

Jack wasn't pleased, not so much because his mother hadn't come, too, but because he and Clive were in the middle of a game with Clive's Hornby train set, which *had* been in that box on top of his wardrobe. The 'Royal Scot' had to go round the track thirty times from London to Weston-Super-Mare, and it was Jack's turn on the transformer, stopping the train at the little station every six times round for people to get on and off at Reading, Swindon, Bath, and Bristol; Clive had looked them up on a timetable. Shirley and Wendy were up at the table in the dining room playing with the model theatre – although when Jack put his head round the door Shirley hadn't sounded as if she was enjoying it very much: 'Can't they do a dance instead of just talking?' she was whining.

Now Ivy Filer was in the hallway. After some tears and handshakes the colonel had gone, driven Parker to the railway station to make sure he went on the

London train; and Lady Ashwell was writing a letter to the Ministry of Food to warn them about the meat rationing racket Eva Hunden had been plotting.

'Oh, my good God!' Ivy Filer was in the hallway crying at the sight of Shirley as Jack came down the stairs. 'Look at the state of you!'

'You should've seen her Thursday,' he said. 'She's a queen to that!'

There were hugs and a bit of crying going on, and Shirley was putting on her drippy look as if she was home already. Then it was cups of tea, and buns, and thank-you's – but not to Jack.

'Shirley's very welcome to stay on here,' Lady Ashwell told Ivy.

'It's kind of you, missus, but she won't, thanks. It's quiet as the grave in London, an' I'm having her home with me. I've made up my mind. There's a train at half-past five, and a bus goes from up the top at ten to …'

'Oh, we shan't have that.' Lady Ashwell offered some more buns. 'I shall take you in the Morris. I didn't drive an ambulance in 1918 for nothing …'

Suddenly, for some reason everyone was looking at Jack: Ivy, Lady Ashwell, and especially Clive.

'*What?*'

'What you gonna do, Jack? Ivy asked. 'Your mum says I can fetch you if you like.'

'Do you want to throw your things into your suitcase?' Lady Ashwell asked, but kindly, not in a hassling way.

Jack looked at neither of them. He looked at Clive – who wouldn't look back at him; he sat there with his hands flat on the kitchen table, his head down above his bun, his eyes squeezed closed, like someone in class trying to remember the words of a poem.

'Can I come to the station?' Jack asked.

'Of course. But bring your gas mask. If you want to go home we can always send on the rest of your things. But remember, you're one of the family here.'

She'd said that twice now – and it wasn't often that Jack didn't know what he was going to do next. Usually he was like quicksilver at choosing a direction. If he'd been asked if he wanted to go home when he'd first come here he'd have known straight-off what to say; he'd have gone back to London like a shot. It had been his first plan, because Union Street School was down in Mardenhurst, and it was closed back in Woolwich. But right now he wasn't so sure. He never did much thinking about himself and how up or down he felt. He just *was*. But now he was being forced to make up his mind in a hurry. Well, it would be good to see his mother again; but he'd had some adventures down here, hadn't he? And old Clive was more of a mate than anyone he'd ever had in Woolwich …

'How long 'fore you go?' he asked Ivy.

Ivy looked at Lady Ashwell.

'In about half an hour,' Lady Ashwell said.

Clive still had his eyes closed, so Jack looked at Wendy, but her head was down into her book of plays.

'I'll definitely come to the station,' he said.

Everyone started shuffling. Florrie patted Shirley's hair, and Lady Ashwell and Ivy stood up. So did Jack. Only now did Clive look at him – with a long, long, stare.

'I'm going for a ride on my bike,' he said – something Jack knew he couldn't do, too, unless he borrowed Wendy's. Clive stuck out his hand to Jack. 'I'll say cheerio, then.'

'I'm only going to the station.'

'Yes. Only to the station.' But Clive's voice sounded as if it came from a long way away. He shook Jack's hand and got up and went towards the scullery and the bike shed – whistling 'Pack Up Your Troubles' as he went.

Lady Ashwell was a good driver for a lady, Jack reckoned. She made a bit of gearbox noise but she didn't crash into anything, and when she stopped at the station Ivy didn't quite hit her head on the windscreen.

Wendy hadn't come, and, of course, Clive hadn't. Jack and Shirley had sat in the back, Shirley with the suitcase the billeting officer had brought to the Hall, and Jack with his gas mask and a couple of things in his raincoat pocket. Just in case. A couple of people got off the train and Ivy opened the door of an empty compartment. 'In you get,' she told Shirley – who did as she was told. 'But if you're coming,' she said to Jack, 'remember you 'aven't got a ticket, I'll have to sort it at the other end.'

'Never been no problem before,' he said. He stood there on the platform and turned to face Lady Ashwell; but he wasn't looking at her, he was looking beyond her to the road – which was empty apart from the Morris, empty as far as the eye could see. 'Ta ever so much,' he said. Right up until that moment he hadn't known what he was going to do. Now he shook her hand and climbed into the train after Ivy. 'Ta.' He hung over the door, with the window right down. ''S'been good.'

'It's been good having you, Jack. It's done Clive a world of … well, it's changed him,' Lady Ashwell said.

Jack hung out of the window and looked along the train. The guard waved his green flag. They were just about off. He was going back to Woolwich, to his mother, and to no school for a good long time. When suddenly he saw him: Clive on his bicycle, riding fast along the road towards the station.

Jack waved. 'Clive!' he shouted.

The railway engine started to chunt, and the carriages jerked forward.

Clive dumped his bike and climbed over the fence onto the platform and stood to attention. He stared at Jack. 'Cheerio, Musketeer!' he shouted. 'Remember always – "One for all and all for one!"' And he saluted smartly, a soldier's stiff salute to an officer. 'Spiffo!'

And in an instant that carriage door was open and Jack was off the train and landing on the platform. He stood up straight and took a good deep breath so as to be heard by everyone.

'Give my love to Ma!' he shouted back at Ivy – before running across to Clive, to go back with him to the Hall, where he would take the two silver dessert spoons from his pocket and put them back where they belonged, in the dining room cutlery drawer.

ABOUT THE AUTHOR

Bernard Ashley lives in Charlton, south-east London, only a street or so from where he was born. Bernard wrote throughout his career as a teacher and headteacher and is now writing full time.

He has written more than twenty full-length novels for young people – and over fifty books in all including picture book texts. He has written television serials including 'Running Scared', 'Dodgem', and the one-off 'Justin and the Demon Drop Kick'.

Bernard is particularly known for the vivid way he reflects our multi-cultural cities, and many of his books have been short-listed for prizes.

He is a popular visitor to schools and libraries, performing lively sessions for children of all ages.

You can visit Bernard on his website at www.bashley. com

Also by Bernard Ashley
available from Ashley Chappel Productions

YOUR GUESS IS AS GOOD AS MINE

'It was screams and running feet all along the street. So it seemed too good to be true when Nicky thought he saw his dad's yellow Mini outside the school.'

But it wasn't his dad's car – and Nicky is suddenly plunged into a terrifying adventure and a frantic race against time …

A rare fiction title on 'Stranger Danger' by the award-winning writer.

'This crisply written book should be on the list for all young readers … a first rate story.' Junior Bookshelf
'An important book for today's children.' Clare Rayner, GMTV

JUSTIN AND THE DEMON DROP KICK

Trouble caught up with Justin on a regular basis. But this was different. All Justin wants is to play football but trouble seems to get in the way. Now someone's kicked a football in Mr Branston's face and the finger's pointing right at Justin.
How can he tell them who really did it?

'Bernard Ashley time after time delivers, really delivers …' School Librarian

HERO GIRLS
Girls who make a difference

Actions speak louder than words!

Say hello to Nerissa, Kompel, Milly, Ugaso and Kim, each a hero in her own way.

Whether it's saving the day at a wedding, helping out a troubled pupil at school or overcoming a personal plight, each of our girls rises to a serious challenge.

Bernard Ashley has created quirky and engaging characters who are joined in this edition by Milly Webster in an exciting new story, 'Stronger then Sprite'.

'Each story is a small, complete piece of drama set in a perfectly realised world of school, classmates and family that will be familiar to readers, making the protagonists immediately recognisable and sympathetic, despite their very different backgrounds ... This is a book that will be enjoyed as well as one that will provoke thought and debate, and it deserves a place on every school and library bookshelf.' Books for Keeps